BONES OF
CONTENTION

A police doctor is out on a limb

CANDY DENMAN

THE
BOOK
FOLKS

Paperback edition published by

The Book Folks

London, 2023

ISBN 978-1-80462-138-7

www.thebookfolks.com

BONES OF CONTENTION is the seventh novel in a series of medical crime fiction titles featuring medical examiner Dr Callie Hughes. More information about the other six books can be found at the end of this one.

Prologue

She stands at the window, looking out across the Old Town. Her straight, blonde hair shining in the light of her living room. She smiles, and for a moment I wonder if she has seen me, but if so, why smile? I crouch down further, just in case, and look around. It's a dark night with no streetlight nearby and there is intermittent cloud covering the moon. I check my position again. I am hidden by some bushes on one side and with the wheelie bins in front, plus I am wearing black clothing. The only part of me that might have been visible to her is my face, but in this dim moonlight she could only have seen it if I moved, which I hadn't, I was sure. No, she couldn't see me here. But what if she did? Would she be pleased? No, I knew she would not. She wouldn't smile, she wouldn't welcome me being here; I knew that and I enjoyed the feeling. She would call the police if she knew, if she knew how I felt about her. I check around me again to make sure I am safe where I am, hidden from her view. Satisfied, I look up again and see that she is still looking out of the window, then she laughs and turns away. She must be talking to someone who is there, in the room with her. I am disappointed, frustrated that I cannot do anything now, tonight. If she is not alone, I will have to wait. It isn't worth the risk. I don't want a witness.

Chapter 1

The location Callie had been given by the police was the end of a row of post-war, semi-detached ex-council houses set back from Harold Road. The house had been recently painted a fashionable pale grey and the front garden was neat and tidy. Callie had walked from the surgery because it really wasn't far and it would have been further for her to walk home and collect her car, but her medical bag was beginning to feel heavy and a slight drizzle had begun almost as soon as she'd started out. At least she was wearing a waterproof jacket and sensible-ish shoes.

Callie was wondering about the reason for the call-out as she approached the house which itself was easily identified by the police constable standing at the front door. All the sergeant on the phone had said to her was that some bones had been dug up. She looked to her right where, beyond the old rectory, All Saints Church was located, surrounded by ancient, lichen-covered gravestones, not in regulated rows like the main cemetery outside town, but untidily crooked and leaning in all directions. Like a graveyard should be, Callie thought; perhaps the bones had come from there. That, or they were from some long-forgotten pet. A small group of people had gathered in the road outside the house, watching what little was going on. With luck, if the rain got heavier, they would go away.

"Dr Hughes." Callie introduced herself to the police officer at the door and he handed her a rapidly dampening clipboard for her to sign in.

"You might want to get a waterproof cover of some kind for that," she told him and he nodded, but did nothing.

"If you could go around the side, Doctor," he said, pointing to a gate.

Acutely aware of all the eyes following her every move, she went through the gate, pulling it shut behind her, and walked down the side alley between the house and the rectory next door and into a back garden that looked more like a building site. A small digger was silent and still, sitting in a patch of mud slightly lower than the lawn. A couple of men in labourer's clothing were standing under a gazebo, smoking cigarettes and trying to keep dry. They looked more disgruntled than interested in what was going on.

Inside the house, Callie could see a heavily pregnant woman who was holding a toddler balanced on her hip. Callie could see another police officer was with her and trying, unsuccessfully, to get her away from the open patio doors.

"Dr Hughes?" a voice said, and she turned to see a uniformed sergeant whom she recognised from her many visits to the custody suite. Her role as a police doctor often meant she was asked to examine both those in custody and police officers who had been injured arresting them.

The rain was getting more persistent and water dripped from the sergeant's cap as he came towards her from the other side of the building work. "I'm Sergeant Bracewell, it was me who called you. Good of you to come out so promptly." He pointed at the place where the digger had been working. "If you could just confirm whether or not these bones are human?"

She looked at the churned-up mess, and sighed. There was nothing for it, she was going to have to get muddy. She went over to the gazebo and the smoking men shuffled up to give her room to put down her bag. She pulled on her crime scene coveralls, some overshoes and gloves, hoping that they would at least protect her clothes from the worst of the dirt as well as protecting the earth, and any evidence it might contain, from her.

Stepping into the newly dug out area, she looked at where the sergeant had pointed. Sticking out of the mud about eighteen inches below the surface was a broken bone that might, or might not, have been a humerus or femur from a person or some other animal. It was too large a bone to be a cat, or a dog, unless it was an extremely large one. A bit further along, she could see a vertebral arch just visible in the dirt. Again, the size could be consistent with a human, she thought. So far, there was nothing absolutely conclusive to tell her what the bones had been or who they belonged to. Callie looked up at the digger bucket and gently moved some of the clod of earth it had just excavated to one side. Underneath it there was a smooth, curved surface of bone visible. Trying to disturb things as little as possible, she scraped some of the earth away until she was sure. As careful as she tried to be, a large clod suddenly dislodged and revealed exactly what it had been covering. It was a skull.

She turned to Sergeant Bracewell.

"They're human," she said, although, as he had been carefully watching her and had seen as much as she had, he had his phone in his hand and was already making the call. There was a sigh from one of the workmen and then they all looked up as someone screamed.

Chapter 2

Callie was sitting on the sofa in the main living-room of the house. She had hurried inside as soon as the woman had screamed, only stopping to remove her footwear at the door. It seemed that living next door to a graveyard was one thing, but skeletons in the garden was a step too far for the householder.

"It was a skull," the woman sobbed. "In my garden!"

"Yes, yes it was," Callie said as soothingly as possible. There was no point denying it under the circumstances, but her voice had the required effect and the woman was now making a little less noise as she cried and the toddler clinging to her gave Callie a serious look. He seemed, quite rightly, to blame her for his mother's distress.

"Here you are," Callie said.

PC Abi Adeola, the officer who had been left looking after the expectant mother and her child, had brought in a tray of tea. Callie picked up a mug labelled 'World's Best Mum'. That one was definitely not for her and she quickly put it back and took the mug with pictures of cartoon cats on it for herself.

"This one's yours, Mel," Adeola said to the woman and, indicating the plate of custard creams on the tray, added, "Maybe you should have a biscuit as well, keep your blood sugar up."

Having missed lunch herself, Callie couldn't have agreed more and the little boy seemed keen as well. He loosened his stranglehold on his mother and reached out, challenging them to stop him as he did so. No one objected and he successfully grabbed a biscuit and shoved it in his mouth as quickly as he could. Callie knew exactly how he felt.

"Is your partner here?" Callie asked gently.

"Neil works in London," Mel replied with a sniff. "He's on his way, said he'd come back as soon as I rang and told him about, about, that…" She waved at the garden.

"That's good," Callie said. "How far on are you?" She pointed at Mel's bump and then allowed her hand to stray over the biscuit plate and snaffle one for herself.

"Eight months. This was to be our forever home. Me, Neil, Archie and Lulu," Mel sobbed. The toddler looked every inch an Archie so Callie presumed that Lulu was the baby bump.

"And it still can be," PC Adeola said soothingly.

"No, no it can't," Mel disagreed. "Not after that." She gestured vaguely in the direction of the garden.

"Just give us a little time to find out what's happened," Adeola told her. "It might just be a mistake, someone buried in the wrong plot, or something. Nothing for you to worry about."

Callie was about to contradict her, after all, there hadn't been any sign of a coffin, but Adeola was giving her a 'keep quiet or else' look and as her reassurance did seem to have quieted Mel, for the time being at least, Callie was happy to leave the consoling role to the police officer.

"Do you have anywhere you can go and stay? Your mum's perhaps?" Adeola was asking as Callie wandered over to the French doors, where she watched Colin Brewer, the civilian crime scene manager, taking control of the scene. He was in full protective gear, quite rightly treating the garden as a crime scene until he had evidence to show that it wasn't. He was taping off the immediate area around the bones to prevent anyone accidentally stumbling into the mess of churned-up mud and destroying the scene, or damaging themselves. A colleague was busy unpacking a forensic tent to protect the area against the rain and the prying eyes of neighbours.

There was a knock on the front door and Callie turned back to the room, watching as Abi went to see who it was, returning a short while later with Detective Sergeant Bob Jeffries.

"Watcha, Doc," Jeffries greeted Callie as Adeola hurried out to fetch another mug of tea. The ageing DS turned to Mel, rightly deducing that she was the house owner. "Mrs Mitchell? I'm Detective Sergeant Bob Jeffries. Are you okay if I ask you a few questions?" Not waiting for an answer, he sat down in the seat Adeola had just vacated as Mel nodded uncertainly and looked at Callie.

"I'll stay if you want," Callie said and came and sat down next to her before turning to Jeffries to explain. "Mel's a bit upset about it all." She silently cursed the fact that Jeffries had been sent rather than someone who might have been more sympathetic, not to mention sensitive, to a heavily pregnant woman's hormonal state.

"Yeah well, no one expects to find bodies under the patio, do they? Not unless they put them there themselves, of course," Jeffries said, gratefully accepting the mug of tea he was handed and ignoring the black looks that both Adeola and Callie were giving him.

"I just wanted a nice garden," Mel wailed.

Jeffries looked surprised by this reaction. He waited until the noise had died down a bit before asking his next question.

"How long have you lived here, Mrs Mitchell?"

"A year ago. We moved in just after Archie's first birthday," Mel said. "We were in a one-bedroom flat so needed the extra space as we were planning on having another baby."

Just then there was the sound of a key in the lock and Mr Mitchell arrived home. Mel leaped up and rushed across the room to throw herself into his arms.

"It's awful, Neil, there are bodies buried in the garden, *our* garden."

"It's okay, it's okay," he said soothingly as he stroked his wife's back and she sobbed into his chest. "Is one of you going to tell me what on earth's going on?" He looked accusingly at Jeffries.

"Mr Mitchell, hello, I'm Dr Hughes," Callie said as she approached him, anxious to get in before Jeffries said something inappropriate, like he usually did. She was very conscious of the fact that she had a blue Tyvek coverall on, and only socks on her feet. She felt distinctly unprofessional and definitely at a disadvantage.

"Is everything all right with the baby?" he asked, panicked by the fact that a doctor had been called.

"Yes, the baby's fine, as far as I know. I'm here because of my connection with the police rather than because your wife is pregnant," she reassured him. "But perhaps it would be better if Mel had a lie-down as she is finding this all a bit upsetting."

"Of course," Neil said and then pushed his wife away from his chest a little. "Mel, shall we go upstairs so you can rest?" he said very gently and tried to walk her to the hall where the stairs were, which was hard with Archie holding on to his leg. "Be a good boy and let me take Mummy upstairs for a nap, okay?" he said to the boy, who seemed reluctant to let him go. "I'll come down in a minute, I promise." He gave the boy a little push towards the lounge.

"Thank goodness for that," said Jeffries. "Never know how to deal with hysterical females. Give me an aggressive drunk any day of the week."

"I'll go outside and see how they are getting on there," she said, pulling on her boots and overshoes, and heading back out into the garden.

The workmen had all gone, presumably having realised that there was no way they were going to be allowed to continue the job any time soon, but the tent was up and there were flashes from inside. Callie poked her head in and saw that the crime scene photographer was busy taking photographs of the bones sticking out of the mud, as Colin Brewer watched.

Leaving them to it, Callie looked down the garden towards the back, expecting to see the churchyard beyond, but instead there were trees and a steep slope up to the cliff top. The rain seemed to have stopped for now and she walked to the rear of the small garden. Standing on tiptoe, she peered over the fence, taking a good look in all directions. Mostly, it seemed to be waste ground, covered in scrub and dying brambles, with a few trees clinging onto the side of the hill. Between the graves in the churchyard and here, there was the walled garden of the old rectory. Of course, a fox or some other scavenger could have dug up the bones and carried them to the garden, but if so she would have expected them to be more scattered. All in all, she didn't think animals were to blame. She walked back to where Brewer was now working through the mud in the digger bucket.

"How's it looking, Colin?" she asked as he carefully placed the skull, still largely covered in mud, into an evidence bag.

"Hard to say how old it is," he told her, "so we're waiting to hear if we can excavate the area or if we have to wait for an archaeologist to come and do it. Not much else we can do until then." He paused as Mike Parton, the coroner's officer, walked towards them, dressed in a Tyvek scene-of-crime suit over his usual dark grey one; she could see the top of his customary black tie at his neck.

"Good morning, Mike," Callie said as Brewer handed over the evidence bag containing the skull.

"Thank you, Colin, and good morning, Dr Hughes." He held up the bag. "Just going to take this to the university. See if we can get an approximate age on the bones before Colin goes any further." He turned and left them, carefully holding the bag away from his body and treating it with great respect, even if the skull's owner was way beyond caring.

Brewer finished making sure that the larger area around where the bones had been found was clearly taped off and attached one end of the tape to the digger.

"So that they can't decide to move it," he explained to Callie.

"You think they'd try and carry on with this job?" she asked, surprised.

"No," he said with a shake of his head, "but I do think they might want to shift this equipment to another site sharpish. They won't want it stuck here for days."

Callie had some sympathy. Diggers weren't cheap and the builder might well need it on another site before too long.

"Right, that's as much as I can do for now" – Brewer disturbed her thoughts as he followed in Parton's footsteps and walked towards the gate – "always best to get an expert opinion before you act."

Callie couldn't agree more.

"Oi! Where's he going?" Jeffries called from the French doors as Brewer hurriedly disappeared around the corner of the house.

Callie didn't want to shout, so she walked towards him, acutely aware of the net curtains twitching in the upstairs windows of the next-door house. She thought they'd probably invited friends and family round to watch what was going on. Besides, she wasn't sure if Mel's bedroom overlooked the garden and didn't want to disturb her.

"The skull has gone to the university to get an opinion on its age," she explained quietly.

"Does that mean they can get on with the patio?" Neil Mitchell asked from behind Jeffries.

"Unfortunately not, Mr Mitchell. Everything must be left untouched until we hear whether the archaeologists or the police will be in charge of collecting the bones."

"I'll be off until we know then," Jeffries said. "The boss will want briefing." He looked meaningfully at Callie.

"I really don't think there's much I can tell him," she replied.

"Well, you can be the one to tell him that then," Jeffries said as he turned to Adeola. "You stay here then, love, hold the lady's hand while I go and break the bad news."

Adeola didn't say anything about being called 'love' by Jeffries but her face spoke a thousand words.

"This is a bloody nightmare," Neil said.

That was something they could all agree on.

* * *

As Callie came through the gate, she could see that the constable who had signed her into the location was speaking to several bystanders. Or rather, that several bystanders were speaking to him and he was looking a little harassed. The rain stopping meant that the numbers had multiplied considerably.

"What's happened?" a thin, well-dressed elderly lady asked him. "It's not the little one, is it?"

"I knew there was something wrong with that family," another answered her.

"Dr Hughes?"

Callie heard her name being called and turned to see one of her patients, an ample middle-aged woman with an underactive thyroid. Despite racking her brains, Callie couldn't for the life of her remember the patient's name, so she tried to just give her a small wave of recognition and escape, but her patient wasn't having any of that. Having made herself the centre of attention by actually being able to address one of the protagonists by name, she wasn't going to let her go.

"Dr Hughes, what on earth is going on? Terry" – she waved towards the house two doors down – "Terry said he could see that the builders had dug up a skeleton. Is that true?"

"Have they built these houses on a graveyard?" A thin, tremulous woman Callie didn't recognise asked, clutching at her oversized handbag.

"I really can't say anything at this point. You will all have to be patient," Callie said firmly and tried to move forward.

A solidly built man in an anorak saw her and stood in her way.

"Stand back," the police officer said, and pushed the man in the chest, in an ineffectual effort to move him.

"What's going on?" He leant towards her, Callie got a waft of bad breath and body odour and took a small step back.

"I'm sorry, you will have to wait and–"

"We have the right to know!" someone shouted from the back, and there was a bit of jostling and jeering.

"Are we in danger?"

"Are the kids in danger?" a woman asked.

"Anyone lays a finger on mine they are dead meat, so help me God!" another said, turning to her neighbours who nodded their approval.

Callie tried to calm the crowd down. "No one is in any danger."

"You heard what the doctor said. Nothing that you need worry about, now move on, please," the officer told the crowd as Callie tried to move quickly past. She was stopped by the police officer himself, who held out his clipboard and she belatedly realised she needed to sign out. Cursing the fact that she had missed her chance to get away, she did so quickly and tried to leave again.

A bigger crowd was beginning to gather, attracted by the first group. Having started off curious, they were now angry, demanding to know what was happening, why the police were there.

"If you could let me get by, I have to get back to the surgery," she said but there was no way she could get through the mass of people.

"Has someone been killed?" she was asked by a woman who seemed excited by the thought, rather than worried.

"Please!" Callie almost shouted as she was jostled. "Let me through."

"Are they paedos?" someone shouted.

"Please!" Callie said again, but no one seemed to be listening to her.

Suddenly, with a bit of pushing and shoving and the occasional "Oi! Watch it!" someone cleared a passage through and held his arms out to give her space.

"Let the doctor get by," he said, loudly and authoritatively, taking charge and holding people back. She looked up gratefully and saw a man in his fifties, dressed in a raincoat, buttoned up to the throat.

"Mr Stenning," she said in relief, recognising a local resident who often helped out with the elderly, running errands and doing their shopping. He had stretched out his arms and cleared a way through the crowd for her. "Am I pleased to see you. Thank you."

"No problem, Doctor."

"Perhaps you should call for some backup," she told the beleaguered policeman and saw him grab his radio as she hurriedly moved away and made sure she was a good distance down the road before turning to look back.

Stenning was standing next to the anxious mouse of a woman who had been clutching her handbag. She was probably the same age as the man, Callie thought, but looked much older, with her wispy hair pulled back into a ponytail and some very old-fashioned clothes hanging off her scrawny frame.

Callie could hear the crowd's anger building and Stenning and the anxious lady were quickly surrounded. She bit her lip and hoped they were all right. It shouldn't be long before help arrived and dispersed the crowd, she told herself. They would be fine.

Once Callie had reached the main road, she turned to see if anyone had followed, but she was alone. She would have liked to thank Mr Stennings properly for his timely intervention, and to be sure that he was okay, but it would have to wait. Perhaps she should call him later.

Chapter 3

When Callie went to the police headquarters to make her report, Detective Inspector Steve Miller was sitting at his desk, wearing a crisp white dress shirt with the sleeves neatly turned up, and a purple and blue patterned tie. He smiled when she and Jeffries walked into the room. It was a smile that she thought, or rather hoped, was more for her than the detective sergeant. It lit up his face and reached all the way to his hazel eyes, or were they amber?

She gave herself a mental shake as she sat in the chair opposite the desk, the only one other than his, so Jeffries was left to lean against a filing cabinet while she filled Miller in on the findings from the garden.

"I'm not sure that these are ancient bones," she said without much preamble. "I don't think you can pass the site over to the university and get them to recover the remains for you, just yet. Mike has taken the skull to the forensic archaeologist there who will be able to tell you more."

Miller's face fell as he registered what that would mean: they would need to treat it as a crime scene until they were sure it wasn't. It was going to need a lot of man-hours to dig up the garden and Callie knew that Miller would be thinking that his annual budget forecast was going to be blown out of the window. His smile had gone and he wiped his face with one hand and sighed.

"How old do you think they are?" he asked.

She wished she could say, but all she could do was shrug.

"I honestly don't know, I'm not an expert on decomposition, but they are definitely human and probably less than twenty years old. You'll get a more accurate answer from the expert."

There were furrows across his forehead as he concentrated on what she was saying, and his eyes clouded as he tried to work out what sort of investigation was going to be needed. She knew that burglary and drug crime were escalating rapidly in the town, as might be expected with the cost-of-living crisis, but she also knew that Miller was newly single and it didn't take a detective to notice that he wasn't looking after himself. There were dark rings under his eyes, and he looked tired. She felt sorry that this was adding to his worries, but there was nothing she could do about that, so she left him to start making the phone calls that would get him the staff and budget he was going to need, if he was lucky.

* * *

"When will they know how old the bones are?" Kate Ward asked as they settled on her comfortably saggy sofa that evening.

"I've no real idea," Callie told her best friend, carefully moving a pile of papers off the only coaster she could find before putting her cup of tea down. The numerous ring marks covering the table were proof that Kate wasn't always as careful as her visitor. "Carbon dating is the most accurate way, but that takes a couple of weeks or more and is expensive, so they won't do that until they have more of an idea. I'm hoping the experts at the university will be able to give us a rough idea of their age in the next few days."

"But you said the bones were in good condition, so they can't be that old, can they?"

"Yes, they were and no, I don't honestly think they can be particularly ancient." Callie had been worrying about that. "So much depends on conditions," she explained to her friend. "In fertile, damp soil, bones would take about twenty years to decay, but in dry conditions they can stay intact for hundreds of years."

"But these were in fertile soil, weren't they? Someone's back garden, under the lawn? Presuming they water it and given the amount of rain we get, it would hardly be dry."

"I know."

"So, do you think they've been there less than twenty years?"

This was what was worrying Callie.

"It's possible," Callie agreed, wishing she could be certain. "Maybe even probable, and that's what I told Steve. I just worry that if I'm wrong, I've given him a whole lot of grief, not to mention trashed his annual budget, for nothing."

"Better to err on the side of caution than end up with archaeologists trampling all over a crime scene, though."

"I don't think archaeologists would trample anything; they are much too careful, unlike some policemen we know," Callie replied with a smile. "But yes, it would be much worse to get it wrong that way round. I just wish I knew more about how long a body takes to decompose, but everything I've read emphasises how complex it is. Soil, water, temperature, whether the body has been embalmed or is in a coffin, these things all affect the calculation." But she hadn't seen any signs of a coffin, and embalming would have preserved the flesh as well, wouldn't it? It was all way too complex.

"Could this simply be a burial that missed the graveyard? Or where the graveyard boundaries have changed?" Kate cut into her thoughts and she came back to the present with a jerk.

"I don't know," Callie admitted. "Bodies were sometimes buried outside the churchyard, in unsanctified ground, if they had committed suicide, but…"

"You don't think these bones belong to one of those?"

"No," Callie told her, suddenly more sure of herself. "They were newish bones, and there was no sign of shrouds or coffins that I could see."

"They could be there, still hidden under the earth," Kate countered, always good at playing devil's advocate.

"No, the bones certainly weren't in a traditional coffin," Callie insisted. "There would have been some sort of trace if there was one, and they were buried in too shallow a grave."

"Any dental work?" Kate asked. "That always seems to help TV detectives."

No," Callie said as she closed her eyes and pictured the skull, sitting in the digger bucket, "there were no teeth that I could see at all."

"Do you do think it's a murder victim, then? Buried in their own back yard?" Kate was leaning forward in her seat. As a solicitor who specialised in crime, albeit petty crime, she had a great interest in the more lurid cases Callie dealt with.

"It could just be an unlawful disposal of a body," Callie said cautiously. "There's nothing to say this John or Jane Doe was murdered."

"Yet," Kate said, with a grin that Callie found hard to return. After all, someone had died, and someone, somewhere, might have loved them, once.

Chapter 4

Billy called her later that evening, as he always did, but a phone call was not the same as seeing someone, not even in this day and age of video calls. Zoom didn't put someone in your bed when you needed to be held or give you the feel and smell of your lover. She missed all that terribly, but had no choice but to accept that a call was better than nothing.

In the beginning, when Billy had first accepted the pathology post in Northern Ireland, they had both promised that they would spend alternate weekends in Hastings and Belfast. But it hadn't worked out that way. With both of them juggling busy working lives and on-call rotas, they were lucky if they actually got to see each other in person more than once a month. But at least they could speak, and she could see him as she told him about her day, even if sometimes he almost seemed bored by it.

"I honestly don't think the bones…" She stopped talking as Billy yawned.

"Sorry, you were saying?" He had the good grace to look guilty. Callie knew how busy his work could be, but that didn't stop her feeling just a little put out.

"You could at least sound a little bit interested." She tried not to look hurt.

"Sorry, sorry," he said, holding his hands up. "It's been a long day and I am absolutely knackered."

Callie had to admit that he did look tired.

"Are you overdoing it, Dr Iqbal?" she asked in a mock stern voice.

"Maybe." He smiled and ran his hands through his hair so that it stuck up in little peaks and made him look about twelve. That made her smile, too.

"I'll let you get some sleep then."

After a few more moments of declaring their love and how much they missed each other, they said goodbye and Callie was left with nothing but the silence of her flat. She went over to the window that looked out over the valley. During daylight, she could see along the coast to St Leonards, but it was the view at night that she liked most, with the lights of the Old Town twinkling below her in the valley and the bright lights of the funfair and arcades along the sea front. As she stood and looked out, she registered some small movement out of the corner of her eye. She looked down at the lane below her window, where she thought it had been. Nothing moved. As her eyes adjusted, she saw that she was looking at the small enclosure that held the wheelie bins belonging to the occupants of the converted house where she lived.

The once large family home she lived in had been divided into three flats and was situated right at the end of the lane, with nothing beyond except the country park and the cliffs. She had bought the top floor flat because she had fallen in love with the view from her living room, but also because it was in a quiet and secluded spot, and – the biggest selling point of all in a town renowned for its parking problems – it had its own parking space. She had since had cause to regret its seclusion, but there was no doubt it was in a beautiful location.

She watched the bin enclosure carefully to see if there was any further movement, but there was nothing to see.

"Foxes," she told herself firmly, and closed the curtains before going into the kitchen area, separated from her lounge by nothing more than a breakfast bar, and starting to prepare her dinner. It didn't take long.

Opening the packaging and placing the plastic container on a plate in the microwave was hardly taxing, but she couldn't be bothered to prepare elaborate meals for one. Billy had been the better cook throughout their relationship and in particular when they had briefly lived together. She thought back to that time, when he had been recovering from being stabbed by a woman who had wanted to kill her. She thought about how he had protected her and the many hours he later spent preparing elaborate meals because it was like therapy for him. At least one benefit of Billy being in Belfast was that she had lost all the weight she had put on during his recovery.

While she waited for the microwave to ping, she thought about their future. Was there one? Billy had been in Belfast for a year, despite their plans that it would only be for a short time. She knew that he had to stay there until a suitable post came up nearer to Hastings, but sadly little had been advertised that would suit him. In return, Billy had sent her details of several GP posts in Northern Ireland that he thought she might be interested in, but she didn't want to move there, away from her friends and family. Impasse. He wasn't happy that she wasn't prepared to move to be with him – but it wasn't her who had left Hastings, it was him.

The microwave let her know her dinner was ready and she tipped a rather gloopy mess of pasta onto a plate. She tried to work up some enthusiasm for eating it and decided that adding a few limp lettuce leaves and an elderly tomato wasn't going to help.

* * *

I need to be more careful when I am watching her, she almost saw me tonight. I need a plan, a real plan for what I want to do to her and I don't have much time. The question is what? What can I do? She has destroyed my life and she deserves to be punished for that. And I really, really want to punish her. I can imagine the release it would give me. The release from all this anger that is building up inside, but I need to be careful, I mustn't make matters worse. I don't want it to come back to me. I want to make her frightened. Frightened enough to leave, go away from here, run away and never come back. I want her to find out what it means to lose everything.

Looking at the word carved on her car, makes me smile. I like that. It was a minor revenge for someone but not enough for me, not nearly enough, but I am glad that she has other enemies out there, as well as friends. I trace the word with my finger, it would be a minor, petty irritation for her when she finds it, but I need to do something big, something that will shake her to the core and change her life forever.

How to do that? How to take everything she values and destroy it? I fantasise about it all the time. The anger is building. It's all her fault. Everything that has happened to me. I would like to take her prisoner, cut off her hair, squirt acid in her face... yes! I like that idea. I wouldn't need to touch her but I want to be close enough to see her skin burn, to smell it as it shrivelled, to hear her scream in pain. Yes, that would be perfect. That would make me feel better, I am sure, but she mustn't know it was me, that was the important thing. She must never know. I need to plan my next move very carefully, make sure I can get away with it. I need to wait, I need to plan. It will take time. And while I am doing that, I can watch her and keep the pressure on her, and think about doing something big to hurt her and get rid of this anger before it destroys me.

Chapter 5

Callie liked to walk to work in the morning, provided it wasn't raining too hard. It gave her a chance to prepare for the day. One problem with this was that if she needed to visit a patient, or was called out by the police during the day, she had to hurry back up the hill to pick up her car. There was also the unpredictable nature of the weather to complicate matters, so she kept a change of clothes at the surgery, just in case. Being prepared for the worst did not mean she actually wanted to get wet, so when she looked out and saw the threatening sky she decided that she would take the car.

Her midnight blue Audi TT had been a present to herself when she had got the police doctor post a few years earlier. Not the most practical of cars, it was, however, her pride and joy. She had parked it facing the cliffs and on the opposite side of the road from her flat, which meant that the driver's door was facing a small patch of waste ground next to the bin store. As she walked round the car, clicking the key fob to unlock the doors, she stopped in her tracks. Someone, or something, had scratched her precious car. She took a closer look. This wasn't accidental damage. She was sure it hadn't been there when she parked up, even in the dark she would have noticed it. *Cunt.* The single word, clear and crudely carved, was not easy to miss and she really couldn't believe a fox could spell that well, so that left some malicious person to blame. Who would do a thing like that?

Callie thought back to the movement she had seen out of the corner of her eye the night before. Could that have been someone vandalising her car? Perhaps she should have gone down and checked at the time. Or perhaps not.

She was neither brave nor stupid and had no wish to confront someone who liked to etch rude words on cars. No. She had no idea what she had done to upset this person, or why they had targeted her in this way but it wasn't nice to think about that. It was not a pleasant thought at all. She shuddered. It wasn't just the vandalism, it was the actual word they had used.

The way the car was parked meant that no one would see the damage if they were walking past, but it would be a different matter if she were to drive it to work and leave it in the public car park where they had a concession for staff to park. Everyone would see the word and she couldn't allow that. It was not one she ever, ever used herself. It offended her and it would offend others, and she couldn't let that happen. She would just have to walk and hope it didn't rain.

As she hurried across the country park, instead of taking a moment to enjoy the sea view, or to marvel at the first signs of spring, she couldn't stop thinking about who might have done the damage to her car. It was infuriating and it would take more than seeing the leaves beginning to unfurl or the blossom beginning to appear to make her feel better. At the bottom of the hill, she popped into the café that was conveniently situated almost next door to the surgery. It had become a regular stop for lunchtime sandwiches and breakfast when she needed a sugar hit or had run out of milk. This seemed to happen fairly often.

Armed with a still warm croissant, the smell of which *was* enough to lift her spirits, Callie hurried into the surgery. Perhaps she should tell Miller that someone had vandalised her car? There seemed little point in reporting it to the police in the normal manner, because what did she expect them to do? It was unlikely to be someone deliberately targeting her, she told herself firmly, much more likely just a random act of childish vandalism. But… she had a niggle of doubt. What if she was the target? Best to report it, and then she would need to arrange for the car to go to a garage as soon as possible, because it wouldn't do to drive around with it as it was. Decision made, she went into the surgery, hoping for a coffee and time to eat her croissant before the first patient arrived.

"Good morning, Callie. We've got a few extras that need to be slotted in this morning," Linda the practice manager said firmly, daring Callie to complain. Perhaps she should have bought more than one croissant, or upgraded to a pain au chocolat, she thought with a sigh as she looked at the long list of people she had been allocated that morning. After her hurried departure from the house where the bones had been found, Callie had intended to call Mr Stenning and thank him for helping, but there was no time to do that before surgery. She could see her first patient was already waiting, so it would have to be left until the end of the list, if she ever got to the end.

A lot of consulting was still being done over the phone following the pandemic, which was good in that it meant she could work from home two mornings a week, but that didn't seem to stem the tide of people who still needed to be seen in person. She was even more depressed to see that one of those that Linda had added to the list was Marcy Draper. Marcy was a long-term patient of Callie's and one who most of her colleagues refused to see because she tended to be disruptive. A local prostitute and drug addict, Marcy could indeed be difficult and her language could be colourful at best and pretty offensive when she didn't get her own way. In an effort to stop her upsetting too many patients she was always given a time at the end of surgery when, hopefully, most people would have left.

It had been a few months since Callie had seen Marcy, either in the surgery or the police station where she was often taken when caught soliciting or assaulting one of her clients. How she still had clients, Callie didn't know; perhaps some of them enjoyed her punching and slapping them. The world was full of strange people, she had found.

When Callie had finally got to the end of her main patient list, she buzzed for Marcy to come in. Nothing happened, so she buzzed again, and when there was no response again, went out into the waiting room.

"She's not arrived," Linda said from behind the desk. Normally she would have been upstairs in the office, but one of the receptionists had called in sick, so the practice manager was working from the front desk that morning.

"No surprise there," Callie replied. "I'll go on up and do my paperwork, let me know if she turns up and I'll come on down."

Before starting on her paperwork, she called Mr Stenning. After several rings, the answer machine kicked in and a disembodied voice told her that no one was available to take her call and asked if she wanted to leave a message, which she did, thanking him for his help. Thinking that perhaps a late lunch was the next item on her to-do list, she was interrupted by Linda calling and letting her know that Marcy had arrived.

It was not unheard of for Marcy to turn up hours, if not days late for her appointments. As it was, she was less than an hour overdue this time and Callie hurried down from the office to see her in the consulting room.

"Hi, Marcy," she said and looked closely at her patient. Dressed in a slightly grubby pink Lycra dress that left little to the imagination and shoes that were teeteringly high and strappy, Marcy was clearly dressed for work. She was dragging a shocking pink wheelie bag and Callie could see that her eyes were slightly glassy, suggesting that she was probably already high.

"Hi," Marcy said as she wobbled in and sat down with a bump.

Callie changed her opinion from 'probably high' to 'absolutely wasted'.

"What can I do for you today?" Callie asked her.

"Nothing," she replied. "I'm here for you, Dr Callie, 'cos you're a friend."

"Well, that's very good of you."

"You are my friend, aren't you?"

"Yes, of course, but I'm also your doctor, Marcy, and I can't help noticing that you might have taken something."

"It's 'cos I'm under a lot of stress, worrying about Zac."

"Zac?" There was only one Zac that Callie knew who might have been worrying Marcy – except he was safely in prison. Callie had helped put him there when she gave evidence against him, detailing the injuries he had caused to a friend and colleague of Marcy's to the court. The friend, who was one of several women Zac pimped out, had been wavering about giving evidence herself because she was frightened of him and what he would do to her if she did. After all, he had caused the injuries to her because she had refused to do as she was told, so what would he be capable of if she testified against him? So, despite the promise of support if she did go to court, she had disappeared instead. Neither Callie nor Marcy knew if she was alive and in hiding, or had been found by Zac and was dead. In the end, Marcy had stepped in to describe the attack she had witnessed, which, along with Callie's evidence of the injuries that had been caused, meant he was sent down, despite the victim not being there to give evidence herself. Needless to say, Zac hadn't taken it well.

"He's out," Marcy said. "Can you fucking believe it?" She waved her hands to emphasise her point and managed to knock over the desk lamp.

"No, he can't be," Callie replied, hastily righting it. "He got eight years only–"

"Five years ago."

Could it really have been as much as five years ago? If so, and if he had behaved himself in prison, he might well be getting out about now.

"They'll contact us, tell us the date he's due to be released…"

Marcy laughed, but it wasn't a happy sound.

"He's already out, I've seen him, spoke to him, that's why I'm fucking outta here."

"But he didn't try and hurt you when you met him?" Callie was clinging on to the slim hope that prison had changed him.

"He's not that stupid. We was in the shopping centre with all the security cameras they got there. He'd have been nicked straight off if he'd done anything."

"Oh." Callie wasn't reassured, at all. "So you are going away for a while?"

"Going to stay with a friend in London." Marcy indicated the bag. "Gotta get going, got a train to catch." She grabbed her bag and started to leave, but turned at the door. "Oh, Zac left a message for you, he said to tell you he's coming for ya."

"Really?" Callie tried not to look too worried, even though she could feel panic rising. Zac was a seriously nasty piece of work.

"Yeah. His girlfriend left him when you got him sent down. Took his kid and all. He said it was all your fault and he won't let you forget it. If you've got any sense, Doc, you'll go away too."

As soon as her patient had gone, Callie sat back and thought about what she had been told. Could Marcy be wrong about Zac Tindall being out? She knew that the probation service was supposed to warn you when someone you had given evidence against was being released, but did it always happen? Clearly not. Zac had publicly threatened her and Marcy with all sorts of retribution when he was sent down, so they should have been given a chance to prepare themselves and take precautions when he was released. Suddenly the word scratched on her car seemed much more threatening, and personal. She shuddered. If Zac Tindall was out and responsible for writing it, he knew where she lived. Worse than that, he had presumably been watching her last night.

She picked up the phone.

Chapter 6

"Well, that's not very nice, is it?" Jeffries said as he bent down to get a closer look at her car door.

Behind her, Callie could hear Miller shouting down the phone. To be fair, most of the town could probably hear him.

"You should have let us know he was being released early!" Miller bellowed. "He's already threatened one of the women who gave evidence against him. Don't you think it would have been nice if you'd kept us in the loop so that we could have put some protection in place you, you…?"

Miller turned to look at the car, and Jeffries helpfully pointed to the word inscribed there.

"He's very handsome when he's angry, isn't he?" Jeffries had a twinkle in his eye.

Callie scowled and didn't answer him, even though he was absolutely right. Miller did indeed look handsome when he was angry. It gave his hazel eyes a deeper, more piercing look.

"Tcha!" Miller made a derogatory noise and hung up without saying goodbye to the poor person at the other end. He stomped towards Callie and Jeffries, still glowering attractively.

"Bloody useless bunch of tossers," he said.

"What was the excuse this time?" Jeffries asked.

"He's a changed man, apparently, so he qualified for the earliest release date possible and they didn't believe he was a threat any longer."

"Still supposed to let us know."

"My point exactly and this" – he pointed at Callie's car – "does not suggest that he's changed much at all."

Callie couldn't argue with that.

"Apparently he's staying with his mum." Miller walked back to his car, parked a little further down the road, and Jeffries hurried after him. "Let's go and pick him up for breach of his bail conditions."

"Oh." He turned back to Callie. "Colin's going to send someone up to photograph and print the car when they are free, so you'll have to leave it for the time being." Then, as an afterthought, he added, "Sorry," before turning and walking away.

"Thanks a bunch," Callie said in irritation but he was already starting his car. Jeffries scurried round to the passenger side to get in. Miller turned his car round in the narrow lane. He headed off with a screech of his tyres.

As Callie went to her front door, Mrs Drysdale, the elderly lady who lived in the ground floor flat, opened her door.

"I do hope you are going to get something done about your car, Dr Hughes, I mean, I will have to look at it every time I go to the bins. It's not very nice, is it?"

Mrs Drysdale seemed to think a lot of things were not very nice.

Callie mumbled an apology and refrained from pointing out that she would have to go right around to the other side of the car to see it, and how often did she go to the bins anyway?

She hurried into her own flat, feeling a little guilty that she hadn't explained what had happened, but knowing that would have only given the woman even more to worry about. It wasn't her neighbour's fault that Zac had damaged her car. In fact, Callie had managed to bring trouble to both her neighbours' doors a number of times over the past few years. Perhaps they were entitled to complain. She just hoped that Zac was blissfully unaware that the police were after him already and that they would find him at his mum's house and send him back to prison. It didn't take long for that dream to be shattered.

"He's not here, and his mum says he hasn't been back since he went to prison," Miller told her only a short time later on the telephone.

"And what does his parole officer say about that?" Callie asked, trying to sound calm.

"Not a lot, as he hasn't got around to seeing him yet."

Callie put her head in her hands. So no one knew where Zac was, and he clearly had it in for her. Terrific.

"Can you go and stay at your parents' house? Or with Kate?" Miller was asking, even though he knew very well that staying with her parents in her childhood home would drive her mad in a very short space of time.

"I don't want to put anyone else in danger," she told him. "Not even my mother."

She could hear Miller sigh in exasperation.

"I'll let the shift sergeant know and ask him to send patrols round as often as he can." They both knew that it wouldn't be very often. "And you should try and take reasonable precautions."

"Like what?" Callie tried to keep the irritation from her voice, but failed.

"Like stay indoors, don't go wandering down that lane of yours on your own, after dark. That sort of thing."

"Are you saying that I can't leave my flat after dark?" she asked him. "In case you hadn't noticed, it's getting dark now."

"Of course I'm not saying that," he replied, more than a little irritated with her, "I'm just telling you to be careful, and maybe call for a taxi if you are going out. Is there a firm you usually use?"

"Yes," she replied, knowing that he was right. Until her car had been processed, and the door resprayed, if she wanted to go out, taxis were indeed a sensible precaution.

"Well, make sure you use them and that you recognise the driver before getting into the cab."

The patronising way he was talking to her, even though she knew his advice was sensible, made her want to dash outside and run across the cliffs shouting for Zac to come and have a go if he really wanted to. But even in her angry state she knew that was not such a great idea.

"I promise I'll be careful," she told Miller sweetly and then swiftly changed the subject so that he would stop lecturing her. "Do you have any more information about the bones found in the garden?"

"We haven't got the full analysis yet, but the archaeologist says they are fairly recent and has sent them on to the forensic anthropologists."

"Ah, that's interesting." Callie tried not to sound too excited.

"It's expensive, that's what it is," Miller said morosely. "Colin and his team are going to do the recovery."

That would go down like a lead balloon with the Mitchells, Callie thought.

"Have the family moved out?" she asked him.

"Yes, well, Mrs Mitchell and the boy have. The husband is sticking round to keep an eye on things."

Callie couldn't blame him for that, even if there was little he would be able to do.

"I might take a wander down tomorrow and see how they're getting on," she told him. It would be a welcome distraction from worrying about Zac. She hoped that vandalising her car was enough to make him feel like he had had his revenge, but she rather feared that he would want something more than that. Something more personal.

It seemed that Billy thought so too when he called soon after Miller hung up, and she told him the news.

"Why don't you come over here for a while? Give the police the chance to catch the SOB and you can maybe take a look at some of the job opportunities while you are–"

"It's not a great time to leave." Callie stopped him before he went any further. "Much as I would like to. I've got that GMC hearing. You know the one, about Gerry, the locum GP we had at the practice a while ago."

"Oh God, yes, I'd forgotten all about that. When is it?"

"Next Friday, and I've promised Jessica I will be there to support her."

"He'll get struck off this time, for sure." Billy sounded like he couldn't believe it hadn't happened already. To be fair, Callie couldn't either.

"I sincerely hope so, the man's a menace," she said. "I just wish Jessica didn't have to be there. I mean it's bad enough that he had an affair with a teenage patient but to make her stand up and tell a panel of probably male doctors and lawyers all about it? That's just awful."

"Can she not just put in a statement?"

"I did suggest that, but if they are going to strike him off the register his lawyer has to be able to question his accuser."

"He's not admitting it, then?"

"No, he says it's all a figment of her imagination and he never had sex with her."

"Do you believe that?"

"Not for a minute. I mean, it's not even the first time he's done something like this, is it?"

"That man is an absolute disgrace."

"No argument from me," Callie said.

"Are you thinking that you'll come over once the hearing's out of the way?" Billy asked. "If so I can try and make sure I get some time off."

"Yes, that sounds like a plan." She tried to sound as if she was looking forward to it, instead of worrying that she would spend the entire time defending her decision not to move over and join him. "I'll have a chat with Linda, and make sure I can at least get the weekend off. Any chance of you being able to come over here in the meantime?"

"I'd love to, but it's really busy here," he said. "I'm pulling a lot of extra shifts, trying to get more experience, and I'm doing a bit of research with a GP practice here so it's hard to get away. I really need to concentrate on that for now, but I miss seeing you."

It was the same thing he had been saying for weeks now, whenever she suggested he could come back to Hastings for a visit. It seemed that she was the one expected to do all the travelling, and that was seriously beginning to grate.

"I'll do my best, but you need to try and get here as well."

"I know, I know, it's hard to get away, that's all."

"It's no easier for me."

"Which is why it would be good if you could move over here, be with me all the time. I miss you so much."

But not enough to make the effort to come and see her, Callie thought silently.

Their conversation finished soon after and despite all the *I love yous* and *missing yous* Callie was in a foul mood by the time it did. She went and looked out of the window, looking down at the bins and the spot where her car was still parked, waiting for the crime scene team to come and check it.

As she watched, her landline rang. Callie was tempted to leave it for the answerphone as only her mother used that number these days, and she really wasn't in the mood to speak to her, but after the third ring she relented and picked up the phone.

"Hello, M—" she started but the voice cut in, talking over her, and it certainly wasn't her mother speaking.

"I see you up there, Dr High-and-Fucking-Mighty. Think you're better than me, do you? Well, I see you and you need to remember what I can do. You tell the filth to keep away from my mum, do you hear? If they go round upsetting her again, I'll take it out on you, not your car, all right? I'll carve you up!"

The voice was unmistakably Zac's and he hung up before she could say anything. The day was going from bad to worse.

Callie put the phone down and went to the window, peering into the gloom by the bins and her car, but there was nothing to see. She shuddered and took a deep breath. The thought that Zac might be there, watching her home and watching her, made her mind up for her.

She deserved a bit of pampering and more than anything, she wanted to feel safe. She made a reservation at the best hotel in town, called for a cab, bunged some clothes and other necessities in a bag, turned out the lights and stood by the window, coat on, waiting and watching. She had seen nothing suspicious by the time the taxi pulled up, so she grabbed her medical bag as well as her overnight one and hurried downstairs.

Chapter 7

As Callie walked up All Saints' Street during her lunch break the next day, nervously looking around her for any sign of Zac, she wondered just how long it was going to be feasible to stay at such an expensive hotel. How long would it be until she felt it was safe to go home? So much depended on factors she had no control over: when the police managed to find Zac Tindall, whether or not he had any more plans for her, or if he'd give up once he realised she wasn't at home. Perhaps she should look for a B&B closer to work, or bite the bullet and go and stay with her parents. She would definitely need a car if she did that, because her parents lived in a village several miles from Hastings and there was absolutely no way she could go home with that word on her car door, not if she ever wanted to hear the end of it. She was going to have to stay in a hotel or B&B at least until the car was sorted, or until she gave up and resorted to renting one while she waited.

Kate had been a little cross with Callie for not going to stay at her place when they had talked over the telephone the night before.

"We could have stayed up all night, putting the world to rights," she told Callie.

"That's what I was afraid of. At my age you need plenty of beauty sleep, you know," Callie had replied, but the truth was, she hadn't slept much anyway. Perhaps alcohol would have helped, but she had been to work too many times nursing a hangover in the past and it wasn't to be recommended, not when you didn't know what might be coming through the door. Facing an infected leg ulcer when you were feeling delicate was not an experience she wanted to repeat, so she had stayed put in the hotel and watched trashy television. She ordered room service but then couldn't face the cold, limp and rather tasteless dinner she had ordered, so dined on the complimentary biscuits instead. They had been surprisingly good.

Miller had been pleased she was in a hotel, but angry that she hadn't let the call from Zac go through to answerphone so they would have some evidence to use against him.

"If you don't recognise the number, don't answer," he told her crossly and she agreed, whilst trying to hide her irritation at his preaching.

"Have you managed to trace the number?" she asked, but wasn't surprised to hear that it was from an unregistered phone, after all, drug dealers weren't generally that stupid.

Morning surgery had not been too taxing, thankfully, and she had confirmed that Colin Brewer was hard at work with some of his team in the garden where the bones had been found. Another pair of CSIs would have finished with her car by mid-afternoon and she had arranged for it to be collected by her usual garage as soon as they were done. It would be a few days before anyone got around to respraying the door but at least it wouldn't be parked outside her home for everyone to see. No courtesy car was available under the terms of her insurance, of course, she would have to organise a hire car to cover her for visits to patients and the possibility of having to move back in with her parents. That really would be the last resort, she told herself. She would stay at the hotel for a few days longer and hope that everything was resolved before her money ran out.

Meanwhile, Callie wanted to see how the excavation of the bones was going, so she walked up All Saints' Street to Harold Road. Ahead of her she saw a tall, rather stooped man wearing a raincoat and carrying two bags of shopping walking in the same direction.

"Mr Stenning?" she called and he turned.

"Dr Hughes," he said as he put down the heavy bags. "Thank you for your message, I'm sorry I wasn't in to take it, but it really wasn't anything you needed to thank me for."

"I disagree, you were a real help, and I felt awful leaving you there. I just hope there's not as many people there today."

"You're going back?" He seemed surprised.

"Just being nosy really, going to see how the excavation is going. I'll let you get on, take your shopping home."

"Oh no, my home's in the other direction. I'm just taking these to Mrs Phelps, she can't get out herself anymore, she's eighty-seven and not as steady on her feet as she used to be."

"That's really nice of you, Mr Stenning. It's good to know there's still people willing to lend a hand."

"It's the least we can do."

He looked as if he was about to say more but, feeling that her duty had been done and wishing to avoid him asking questions about the bones, Callie said goodbye.

"Mustn't keep you," she said and hurried on ahead.

There was no longer a crowd outside the house, but she could see someone sitting in a parked car outside the property, presumably a reporter, and as she approached the house, the curtains in the house next door twitched and an elderly lady peered out. She recognised her as the well-dressed woman who had been concerned about 'the little one' and Callie gave her a reassuring smile.

Callie signed into the scene on the clipboard held by the constable tasked with keeping a log of everyone who came into the garden. He looked absolutely frozen, and as Callie went through the side gate, she hoped someone was keeping him well-supplied with hot drinks – the lady next door, perhaps.

In the garden, Callie went over to the forensic tent and pulled the plastic sheet covering the entrance to one side. Brewer, kneeling in the mud was carefully removing blocks of earth from just above the spot where the bones could be seen sticking out.

"Good afternoon, Colin," Callie said as he looked up to see who it was. "How's it going?"

"We're getting there," he replied. "I've just reached the level where the bones are, so you've come at the right time."

He had already excavated an area roughly two feet wide and six feet long and was almost to the depth where the bones were situated. As he removed each clod, he handed it to his colleague and it was then placed in a sieve held over a sheet of plastic and sifted for any artefacts or bones. Anything this CSI found was then placed in a carefully labelled evidence bag detailing the location and what depth it had been recovered from. It was a slow and painstaking way of doing things, particularly in the cold, but it was the best way of ensuring nothing was missed.

Changing his small spade for a trowel and a brush, Brewer began carefully removing the earth around the long bone that Callie had thought might be a femur or a humerus, depending on the size of the person buried. Further excavation made her pretty sure it was a femur as first the ball joint and soon after part of a pelvis were revealed.

It was freezing standing watching them work and Callie looked longingly towards the house.

"He's not in and has left the place locked up so we can't go in," Brewer's assistant told her, bitterly.

"I'll do a café run then," Callie said, "what would you like?"

Having taken orders for hot chocolate, coffee and bacon rolls, and not forgetting to find out what the frozen constable at the gate wanted, Callie went to a local café on the high street to get them. By the time she had returned, put her crime scene suit back on and handed out the lunches, she could see that much of the skeleton had been revealed. While Brewer was standing outside the tent, eating his sandwich, she bent down and took a closer look.

"What do you think, Doctor?" Brewer called to her between mouthfuls. "I was thinking it's an adult male."

Callie took a moment before she answered. "I agree, but what do you make of that, Colin?" she asked, pointing to a nub of bone sticking out next to the pelvic bones. Swallowing the last of his sandwich, he put his gloves back on and crossed the garden to where she was and crouched down beside her.

"Looks like the top of the tibia," he said, concerned.

"Yes, but we already have two tibias completely revealed here…"

"Right," he sighed. "Well, we'll have to extend the excavation site then, won't we? Will you tell DI Miller there's more than one body, or do you want me to?"

Callie agreed to speak to Miller and then checked her watch. She needed to get back to the surgery pretty soon, but she very much wanted to tell him in person rather than over the phone, so it would have to be a quick visit. She wished she had her car with her. If she hurried to the sea front, hoping there would be a taxi waiting at the rank.

* * *

When she arrived in the main CID office, she could see that an informal briefing was in process. Miller and Jeffries were perched on the edge of DC Nigel Nugent's desk, where the nerdy-looking Nigel was reading from his computer screen. DS Jayne Hales had pulled her chair across so that she could see his screen as well.

"What's up?" Callie asked as she came up and unashamedly peered at the screen.

"No record of people being buried outside of the main graveyard right back to the start of records, and no one has applied for a council licence to dispose of a body in that garden, or any other in the area, in the last hundred years," Nigel summarised for her.

"Well, we didn't think this was a legitimate burial because there was no sign of a coffin," Jayne added.

"Could have been an eco-burial, you know, in a wicker basket or cardboard coffin, or something." Nigel seemed reluctant to let the idea go.

"And the body was not buried the regulation six feet down, was it?" Hales turned to Miller to confirm this and he nodded.

"Only a couple of feet, if that, wouldn't you agree?" Miller looked at Callie.

"Yes, I think the uppermost parts of the bodies are only about eighteen inches under the surface."

There was a moment of silence as they processed her wording.

"Bodies?" Miller finally queried.

"Yes," Callie replied. "The first skeleton has been almost completely revealed now, but it seems that there are more bones than there should be so Colin has extended the search area to see if there is a second body."

"That's all I need," Miller said with a groan.

"How sure are you that there's more than one?" Jeffries queried.

"Well, unless the first body is Jake the Peg, with an extra leg, pretty sure," she told him. "Colin was also ordering up ground penetrating radar when I left him. He said they needed to go over the whole garden and see if there are any more bodies anywhere else." She didn't like to imagine what the Mitchells would make of their whole garden being dug up. Not to mention the neighbours.

Miller groaned again. He wasn't happy at this turn of events either.

* * *

She must have moved into a hotel. There is no sign of her at home and so I follow her from the surgery to find out where she is staying. It isn't easy as she walks fast. I am trying to keep well back because she keeps looking around, checking for someone doing exactly as I am, following her, but I don't think she sees me. Even if she did, what would she see? I'm just another bloke with a baseball cap and hoody, there are plenty enough around here. I was close to losing her several times as she walked to the hotel, and, as it is, I am not quite sure where she has gone, as there are several hotels next to each other along the coast road. I stand in the shelter of a doorway and watch them all, hoping to see a sign, anything that will tell me which one she is staying in.

There she is! At a window on the second floor. I almost jump with excitement. She is standing looking out, the room lights behind her, not realising how distinctive she is, how easy to pick out as she peers out into the dark.

Chapter 8

"What about the house owners?" Billy asked when he called later. "Have they been there long?"

"No, about a year, that's all," Callie told him. "And why would they get someone in to dig up the garden for a patio if they'd buried bodies there?"

"Fair point," Billy answered. "What about previous owners?"

"Nigel has a list that he got from the land registry; there's not many, so that should make things easier. It was council owned until 1985, when it was sold to the people who were living there at the time. It's had two more owners since then."

"Sounds like a narrow field then."

"It could be a previous council tenant, of course, and there have been a few over the years apparently."

"Getting the approximate age of the bones should narrow the field down."

Holding her tablet so she remained in the picture, Callie wandered over to the window and looked out. When she had moved into the hotel, she had asked for a sea view, and she certainly had that; the trouble was, it was not as good as the view from her flat, which, being high up, looked towards the sea, over the town. This view, across a small patch of garden to the main road along the sea front, beyond which was the beach, was much more limited and less interesting. She had also found that despite the double glazing, the street noise was quite loud and intrusive.

"Yes, but getting a cause of death is going to be tough," she said as she looked along the sea front. There was a row of cars waiting at the lights, and, despite the dark and the steady drizzle, a few people were still out and walking along the promenade.

"Almost impossible unless they find cuts on the bones suggesting stabbing, or holes in the skull made by a blunt instrument."

"I know," she agreed. "They should be able to get an approximate age of the victims when they died though, which will help."

"What about genetics and chemical analysis? Will Miller stump up for more expensive tests like that?" he asked.

"I think that depends on how far they get using normal channels." They both knew that budgets were tight these days.

Callie's gaze wandered along the length of garden until something caught her eye. A man in a baseball cap and hoodie was standing in the sea view shelter closest to the hotel. The shelters, one at either end of the little patch of communal garden outside the hotel, were concrete and had seats facing in all directions, so that someone could sit and pass the time of day, sheltered from the wind, no matter which direction it came from. Perhaps the man was simply trying to get out of the rain, she thought, but something about the way he was behaving wasn't right. She froze and tried to make out who it was, but he was in too much shadow and with the hoodie and cap, it was impossible. Was he watching the hotel? Was he watching her?

"Hello?" Billy said and Callie realised she had missed something he had said and he would be able to see that her gaze had been somewhere other than at him. "Is everything okay?"

"I'm sure it's nothing, it's just that there's a man across the road and…" She moved the curtain further out of the way and stared at the man, who seemed to notice, slipping further into the shadows.

"He can't have found out where you're staying," Billy said, but even he didn't sound too sure about that.

Callie let the curtain drop. She had made her mind up.

"Bye, Billy. I'm going to check on him."

"Don't!" he shouted but it was too late. She'd chucked her tablet on the bed, grabbed her coat and keys and was rushing out of the door as he finished. "Don't go out there, please, Callie!"

Quite what the receptionist thought was going on as Callie rushed through the lobby and out onto the road, she didn't know, or care.

A car horn blared as someone ran across the road further down the sea front. She reached the shelter and went all the way round, checking each section. It was empty, so she sprinted along the road and crossed at the traffic lights. She looked up and down the promenade, but he had gone, of course. She walked a little further towards St Leonards and looked along the sea front, but it was hopeless and she gave up.

She could hear a siren approaching as she walked back towards her hotel, and a police car screeched to a halt beside her. The driver wound down his window and Callie recognised Sergeant Bracewell.

"Everything all right, Dr Hughes?" he asked as he got out of the car, pulling on his cap to protect himself from the rain.

"I just thought I saw someone watching the hotel where I'm staying, but he seems to have gone."

Bracewell looked up and down the road.

"Description?"

"IC1 male, I think, black or dark blue baseball cap, grey hoodie, dark trousers. Medium build, about five ten or eleven, maybe?"

"I'll circulate that," he said, but they both knew she had just described a large chunk of the population. "How could he have found out where you are staying?"

"I don't know," she admitted. "Followed me, I suppose, or it could just be my overactive imagination." But she didn't think so. Something about the way the man had been standing, half-hidden in the shadows, plus the fact that he had run as soon as she had spotted him, told her that he had been watching the hotel, and her.

"Did Billy call you then?" she asked.

"Dr Iqbal called the station and said you'd gone haring off after your stalker." He smiled as he said it. "So I thought I'd better get over here sharpish."

"And thank you for that. I'd better go and let him know I'm okay," she said.

"Yes," he agreed. "I'll take a drive round, see if I can see him, then stay in the area as much as I can, in case he comes back."

"Thank you." She turned and crossed back over the road to return to the hotel. Her phone rang as she made her way back up to her room.

"Hi, Billy, yes, I'm fine. He was long gone by the time I got down there, and thank you for calling the police out."

There followed a not-unexpected lecture about not rushing off after violent criminals and putting herself at risk.

"I know, I know," was all she said while it was going on, and when Billy had finally finished she tried to change the subject. "Anyway, I'm soaked and I need a shower after all that running. This hotel doesn't run to baths, unfortunately." She hadn't really run all that far, but she didn't want to prolong the conversation any further.

To her surprise she didn't get any of his usual banter or declarations of love, just a rather tired goodnight. The business of her chasing after Zac must have worried him more than he was letting on. But it seemed that it was still not enough to get him to come over to Hastings and be with her. In some ways that was a relief, because she would only end up worrying about him as well, but it niggled, a little, that he didn't even offer.

Once she had showered, and made herself a comforting mug of hot chocolate to drink in bed, she opened her laptop to check emails. There were about forty unread ones and she could never go to bed without clearing her inbox. Not if she wanted to sleep, anyway.

She was pretty strict with herself about not getting bogged down with emails relating to patients; she moved them to a folder that she would deal with next day at work. There was the usual spam that went straight into the recycling bin. Copies of the various magazines such as *Doctor* and *Medscape* went into their respective folders to be read when she had time. Then there were one or two more personal emails from friends and last but not least, one from Dr Gerry Brown's personal email address. The message header was 'please read'. He had been advised not to contact her, but still, he had. The cursor hovered over the delete function, but she would wonder about what it said, so she opened it instead and read the contents.

Please, please stop the hearing. Jessica is lying, I never had an affair with her. I know I messed up in the past and I know I need to do better, but I am not guilty of this! I promise I will not work with women ever again, if you and she withdraw your statements. If I get struck off, it will finish me. Without my work, I have nothing. I couldn't bear it. I will kill myself. Gerry.

She should never have read it. There was absolutely no hope of her getting any sleep now. If the stalker having found her at the hotel wasn't bad enough, now she was going to be worrying about Gerry Brown killing himself if she gave evidence against him. She forwarded his email to Kate. Sensible, pragmatic Kate, who knew her better than anyone else, and knew Gerry as well. Then she closed down her laptop. Should she reply? Tell him about Mr Hemsworth? Or would that only make matters worse? She picked up a paperback she had brought with her, but was too wound up to settle. Fortunately, it was only a few minutes later when her phone rang and she picked it up, expecting it to be her friend.

"Hiya," she managed to say before the person at the other end went off on one.

"What's all this I'm hearing about you chasing after your stalker, on your own and in the middle of the night?"

Callie sighed, she really should have checked the number before answering. DI Miller sounded extremely cross.

It took her a good half hour to calm him down and get him off the phone, by which time her hot chocolate was cold and she had missed a call from Kate.

Making herself a fresh hot drink she snuggled up in bed and called Kate back.

"So, do you think he is suicidal?" she asked her friend.

"What a tosser that man is. Does he really think he can wriggle out of this by threatening to commit suicide? He doesn't have the courage." As usual, her friend was robustly anti Dr Brown; after all, she'd had a run in with him before when they had met on a dating site.

"What if he does, though?" Callie wasn't sure she could live with herself if he committed suicide.

"That's exactly the reaction he's hoping for. Believe me, he knows what he's doing."

Callie had to agree with that, but she still spent the night awake, worrying about whether she would be hounding Dr Brown to his death, or if he was just trying to manipulate her into withdrawing her support of Jessica.

Chapter 9

Callie checked out of the hotel the next morning, as she could see no point staying there if Zac had found her so easily. Even though the bed had been very comfy and the pillows soft, she still hadn't slept well. She was tempted to blame the traffic noise, and other guests stomping up and down the stairs, but she knew neither were the real reason; she had just been too wound up to sleep.

As a result, she was so tired she couldn't think straight and she struggled through her morning work. Not even coffee seemed to help.

At last her list was finished and she grabbed her bag and headed out. Linda was behind the reception desk again, they seemed to be perennially short of help and despite being the practice manager, she ended up covering quite often. Callie waved at her and indicated she was going upstairs for another coffee break.

"I'll bring some down for you too," she said.

Before Callie could even reach the bottom of the stairs, the main door burst open and a muscular man in his forties came into the surgery. He was neatly dressed in chinos and a polo shirt with some sort of regimental badge on the chest. He wore no coat despite the cool weather, meaning that his forearm tattoos were on display.

"Dr Hughes, the very woman I want a word with," he said, pointing at her.

"If you'd like to make an appointment–" Linda began but the man didn't even pause.

"I blame you and the rest of the muppets that work here for what happened to my daughter, for what that bastard did to her."

"Mr Hemsworth–" Callie tried to interrupt and shepherd him into a consulting room, but he was going to say his piece and he wasn't going to let anyone distract him.

"She met him here, and when you found out what was going on, under your noses, you didn't deal with it properly." Another slight pause. His words were threatening, but what made it worse was the icy calm with which he delivered them. "So now my daughter has to stand up and tell the world what he has done to her, something that will break her, and so will break me as well, just because *you*" – he pointed at Callie and then Linda – "and *you*, have not done your jobs."

"To be fair–" Callie attempted to make this a dialogue rather than a lecture but he wasn't about to let that happen.

"So, I want you to let that bastard know that he has to admit everything so that she doesn't have to do that, or I will tear him limb from limb. Got that?"

Callie nodded, but neither she nor Linda said anything as he turned and walked towards the door. Once it closed behind him, Callie let out a breath she hadn't been aware of holding.

"Phew," said Linda. "He's a bit scary, isn't he?"

"You can say that again."

"Rumour has it he was in the SAS."

"I can believe it."

"And he is very protective of Jessica, since her mum died," Linda added. "Are you going to pass the message on to Dr Brown?"

"I'm not supposed to have any contact with him before the hearing," Callie answered. "But I think it's only fair that we let him know Mr Hemsworth is out for his blood, although you'd think that he would have worked it out for himself. Do we have his current contact details?"

"I'll check but he was only in a rented flat after his wife kicked him out, so he might well have moved on, and we took back his work mobile. Won't the GMC have his current address?"

"Yes, but it's them who say I shouldn't contact him. I suppose I could ask them to pass on the message, but it might take days. Can you see what you can do? There's nothing to say the surgery can't contact him."

"Or we could just leave him in the dark and let Lewis Hemsworth beat him up? You know, a bit of rough justice."

Callie rolled her eyes by way of an answer, and headed up the stairs. Gerry Brown had briefly been a locum at the practice, but had a history of getting sexually involved with patients. Callie had reported him a few months after he had joined the team, and he had been suspended as a result. Unfortunately, he had been reinstated when his psychotherapist insisted that he had been successfully treated for his sex addiction. He had not been taken back by the practice, but was working at the hospital which was where he had once again met Jessica, a vulnerable teenager with an eating disorder and a patient of Callie's he had first seen during his time at the surgery. When Jessica had come to Callie for contraception advice and let it slip that she needed it because Gerry was her boyfriend, Callie had reported him again and he was suspended, again. The BMA panel set to hear the case wanted Jessica to give evidence, but clearly it was causing her distress. There was certainly a part of Callie that agreed with Linda, perhaps Lewis Hemsworth should be allowed to beat him up, but she also wanted him to be struck off. He couldn't be allowed to use his position as a doctor to seduce young or vulnerable women again.

She also had to consider his threat to commit suicide. Would the additional pressure of knowing Lewis Hemsworth was looking for blood tip him over the edge? Should she call off the hearing? Could she, even if she wanted to? Or would the GMC press ahead regardless because of the evidence already submitted? Having successfully put the problem out of her mind all morning, and knowing that she could no longer do so, she decided to ask her colleagues what they thought. After all, it wouldn't be good for the practice if Brown killed himself and the papers reported that he had been hounded to death by one of their doctors.

"It is a concern," Gauri Sinha, the senior partner, told her. "It would be an awful thing to have on your conscience, but only you can decide on whether or not to take the risk."

No help there then, so she asked the youngest of her colleagues, a young man not blessed with a great deal of insight.

"I wouldn't top myself if I got struck off, no. I'd take a nice long holiday. Think about it: never having to see a patient again, never worrying about whether or not you'd got it right, no more screaming babies, unless they were your own, of course. What do you think about working abroad? Been wondering about Australia. What's it like there, do you think?"

Making a mental note not to rely too much on him staying, and thinking that maybe they ought to start looking for a replacement just in case, Callie asked Linda what she thought when she finally came up to the office.

"Hard to say, really," she replied nonchalantly. "He didn't strike me as the type to kill himself, he's much more likely to get himself killed. Take this morning, for example. On the whole, I'd favour the 'playing you' point of view. I mean, it looks like it's working, too, but if I can dig out a phone number, maybe we ought to at least give him the heads up about Mr Hemsworth."

* * *

As Callie left after evening surgery, clutching both her medical and overnight bags and wondering if it wouldn't be wiser to call for a taxi, she was surprised to see Kate waiting for her.

"Carry yer bags for yer, luv?" she asked in a fake Cockney accent.

"What are you doing here?" Callie asked with a smile.

"That's nice, I come all the way down here–"

"All of a couple of hundred yards."

"All that bleedin' way, so that I can help you walk back to your flat and what do I get? Nothing but a mouthful of abuse. Ugh, I can't keep up that accent any longer." They both laughed as Callie handed over her medical bag, the lighter of the two she was carrying, and they started off up the steps towards the country park and the path to her flat.

"Why, oh why do we live in such a hilly town?" Kate grumbled as they stopped at the top of the steps while she caught her breath.

"So we don't have to bother going to the gym," Callie answered.

"We certainly do need to go to the gym – it's a great place to pick up men."

"Met anyone interesting recently?" Callie asked as they set off across the grass. Callie was trying to hurry because the clouds were looking threatening and the sky was beginning to darken. She had no wish to get wet, and she was a little apprehensive about arriving home in the dark, even with a friend in tow, but Kate was not one to rush.

"Define interesting," Kate replied.

Callie smiled and took a deep breath of the fresh sea air. This was where she belonged, she thought, here in Hastings. This was home. Darkness was falling fast. It was another week until the clocks went forward to summer time, and Callie longed for the summer evenings, and being able to walk home from work without stumbling in the dark. The country park had no lights, the first street light being the one at the end of her lane, almost outside her front door. She did sometimes worry that she would stumble in a rabbit hole, or trip over a root, and no one would find her until morning.

"Come on, let's get back before it gets too dark," she urged her friend. "There's a bottle of wine in the fridge, just waiting to be poured."

"Now you're talking," Kate replied and hurried after her friend.

* * *

Before opening the wine, Callie closed the curtains, not just in the living room, but in her bedroom as well. She didn't want anyone outside to be able to see where she was or what she was doing.

"Am I coming across as paranoid?" she asked Kate.

"Just sensible," was the firm reply.

Once they both had full glasses, and having placed the bottle within easy reach, Callie sat down with a sigh.

"Do you think I'm being stupid? Coming back here?" she asked.

"I would feel much happier if you had booked yourself on a holiday to somewhere exotic and far away for a couple of weeks to give the police a chance to catch the scumbag and put him back inside, if only for breach of his bail conditions," Kate told her. "Or you could go back to your parents – although I do realise that's not really an attractive option," she added with a smile, "not if you want to retain your sanity. But honestly, I don't know why you don't go and stay with Billy until this all blows over."

"I can't just up and leave work in the lurch."

"Oh, I think you can, under these circumstances."

"And there's the hearing into Gerry Brown, if he decides to turn up for it."

Kate pulled a face at the mere mention of his name.

"Did you tell him about the threat?"

"Linda did, and he told her that he had already heard from Jessica's dad via a contact at the hospital and was staying as far away from Hastings as he could."

"Which is exactly what you should do. Not for good, a week or two should be enough."

"But what if he doesn't admit to having sex with Jessica? What if he just carries on denying it all and blaming her, right to the bitter end? I mean, that would be just like him, wouldn't it?"

"Yes," Kate said. "Yes, it would and I can see that you might want to grab the chance to support her story and get him struck off, but is it worth putting yourself at risk?"

"Maybe not," Callie conceded, "I really don't want to let him get away with it. But…" Was it worth the risk? And the stress?

"And it would be good to see Billy, wouldn't it?" Kate pressed home her advantage, but Callie didn't say anything for a moment or two. "Wouldn't it?" Kate persevered.

"I don't know," Callie replied, doubt clear in her voice.

"What don't you know?"

"There's something… Billy isn't…" she faltered.

"What?"

"I think he's not as keen on me as he was," she explained. "He hasn't been over here in weeks."

"But he's asked you to go over there?"

"Yes, but even with that, he's not as insistent."

"You mean he's not begging for it."

"No, it's not that" – she thought for a moment – "well, yes, actually, it's exactly that. It's as if he's just saying that he wants me to visit because he knows I won't."

Saying it out loud made Callie realise just how sure she was that Billy's love for her wasn't as strong as it had been, and how much it had been preying on her mind. Absence didn't seem to have made his heart grow fonder. Not in his case, anyway.

Before Kate could respond, there was a ring on the doorbell. Callie checked who it was and was surprised to see Steve Miller on the video display.

"Come on up, Steve," she said as she buzzed him in.

"Want me to disappear?" Kate asked, standing up as they heard him coming up the stairs.

"No, no," Callie quickly replied. "It's better that you stay."

"Yeah, we don't want you throwing yourself at him in desperation," her friend said with a wry smile.

"Like I'd do that." Callie dismissed the thought. After all, she said to herself, she might be wrong about Billy's affections, and getting too close to Steve wouldn't help sort their relationship out, or rather, it would, in that it would finish it completely and she wasn't sure that was what she wanted, yet. A part of her did, but another part of her wanted to fight for Billy, get back what they had lost somewhere along the line.

If Steve was surprised to see that Callie wasn't alone he didn't show it. If anything, he seemed relieved.

"Glad you haven't completely lost your mind," was the first thing he said as he came through the door and, as opening lines went, it wasn't exactly friendly. "Why on earth have you come back here?"

"Where exactly do you suggest I stay, Detective Inspector?" Callie replied coldly. "No, wait, I am not going to move back in with my parents," she said, knowing that was exactly what he had been going to suggest. "Nothing is worth having to do that."

"Well, go and stay with friends." He looked at Kate. "Ones that live further away than Kate," he amended.

"Zac didn't take long to find me at the hotel, so how long do you think it would take him to track me down anywhere else? Unless you are suggesting I leave the country like Kate keeps telling me to."

"Well, that would certainly be a good start," he said.

"I am not leaving Hastings," she told them both, and herself, firmly, but Kate seemed to be deep in thought.

"How do you think he managed to find you?" Kate eventually said, pouring herself another glass of wine.

Miller sat down, as both he and Callie thought about it.

"Did you tell anyone you were going to the hotel?" Miller asked.

"No one," Callie answered, and it was true. That was what was frightening. She had told no one she was going there, just booked it, grabbed her things and went. "I booked online, the receptionist obviously had my name, oh, and the taxi driver, but he was my usual firm, and a driver I recognised."

Miller was making notes.

"Taxi company?" he asked. "I'll check them and the hotel receptionist."

Callie felt bad as she was sure neither could have told Zac where she was and now they were going to find themselves persons of interest to the police. She went to fetch another glass for Miller.

"Do you think he's put the word out across the town, asking any of his contacts who see Callie to let him know where she is?" Kate asked Miller.

"None of our sources have indicated that he has. In fact, none of them seem to have seen him at all." Miller poured himself a glass of wine. "At least, they are not admitting it to us."

"If he isn't getting people to tell him where I am, he must be following me." Callie wasn't sure which was worse, the thought that someone had bribed people to watch out for her, or that she was being followed around. "And if he's following me, then it doesn't really make any difference where I go because he will know."

"Unless you went jetting off to somewhere exotic," Kate persisted. "He couldn't follow you then, could he?" She gave Miller a meaningful look. Miller took a gulp of his wine before answering.

"I can put out an alert, to make sure we are told if he does try to follow and leave the country."

"An alert like the one from the parole people that was supposed to warn me that he'd been released?" Callie said with an acid edge to her voice. Neither Kate nor Miller replied; they both knew she had made a fair point. "What are your plans?" Miller asked, not unreasonably.

"I've no idea; just carry on as normal and keep my fingers crossed."

Neither Miller nor Kate seemed overly happy with that idea.

"You could stay with me, I have a spare room, after all," Kate told her.

"No, I'll be fine," Callie insisted.

"Then I will just have to stay here with you, I can sleep on the sofa–" Kate started to say.

"No! I am not having you put yourself at risk," Callie interrupted her.

"You can't stay here on your own," Kate continued in a reasonable voice, refusing to be put off. "I can accompany you to and from work, in a taxi because I'm buggered if I'm going to do that sodding walk every time."

Callie was equally firm in her refusal. "I can't ask you to do that."

"Well, I think that it's a good start if you really won't go away for a while," Miller told her. "I'll bend a few arms and try and get more patrols up here and at your work too.

That will be the easier one to set up, as there are patrols along the sea front anyway."

"And you need to tell them at work that you can't do visits," Kate told Callie.

"I can do them by taxi," she countered.

"No. Kate's right," Miller said. "It would still be way too easy for him to follow you from the surgery."

Callie shivered because she knew he was right. She poured herself some more wine. At this rate she was going to have to open another bottle.

"I was surprised he advertised himself the way he did," she said eventually.

"How do you mean?" Miller asked.

"Well, if he really meant to do anything bad to me, worse than writing rude words on my car, then why was he hanging about outside my hotel? It means I'm on my guard, and you are all watching out for him too. It just doesn't make sense."

"Unless all he wants to do is to scare you," Miller finally said and Callie thought he was probably right. The two incidents were meant to frighten her and they had succeeded.

"Right, that's decided then," he said, although Callie didn't think she'd actually agreed to anything.

However, before she could stop them, Miller was taking Kate's keys from her and agreeing to collect the ready-packed case she had apparently left by the front door of her home. Callie had a growing suspicion that it had all been set up in advance. Out-manoeuvred, she went to fetch the bedding.

* * *

I'm back watching her flat, hidden behind the bin store, looking up at her home. The lights are on and she has closed the curtains, but I can see a little through the window over the sink that she has forgotten. I can see that her so-called friends are there again. I hadn't planned for this. I had always thought she might run, go to a hotel, as she did before. It was easy enough to follow her and find out where she was staying. Not so easy to get to her there though, not with the receptionist watching everyone coming in. So I showed myself, let her know that I can find her wherever she is. I hoped that would mean she came home, and she did.

Now she is back but it seems that they aren't going to let her be alone for a minute. Maybe they will get bored soon. They are bound to need to go to their own homes at some point, aren't they? I need to be patient. That makes me think. What about patients? She can't get out of doing visits forever, I just need to find a way of knowing where or who she is visiting. I need a better plan, and this might be it.

Chapter 10

Callie woke early and crept out of her room. Kate was a heavy sleeper and it would take more than her host moving around and making a cup of tea to wake her. While waiting for the kettle to boil, Callie turned to the kitchen window and fiddled with the blind which had jammed open weeks ago. She kept trying to free it but it was well and truly stuck. Maybe she should give up and get a new one. Looking at the town, people were slowly beginning to wake up. Lights were on, but their yellow glow was less and less obvious as the sky became lighter.

She heard a car door open and looked down to see Miller getting out and stretching. He glanced up and saw her, giving a little wave before getting back in his car and driving off. If Callie had known he was out there keeping watch, and presumably had been all night, she would have taken him a cup of coffee. It was the least she could do, but it was too late now, she had missed her chance. She would have to ring and thank him later, or better still, go and see him, to tell him it couldn't continue. He would be exhausted sleeping in his car and keeping watch over her every night; it was too much.

True to her word, Kate insisted on calling a taxi and seeing Callie safely into the surgery before going on to her own workplace. Callie was overwhelmed by how her friends were rallying round, trying to make sure she was safe. Her colleagues, however, were less accommodating. There was a lot of grumbling from them when they were told that she wouldn't be doing visits for the foreseeable future, and they were only slightly mollified by her volunteering for the weekly baby clinic and some of their repeat prescription duties.

It had been nice having Kate stay over for the night, it had made her feel safe, but Callie liked her own space, and she felt guilty. She didn't relish having her friend, and all her belongings, living with her for long and she knew the sofa wasn't comfy; she'd fallen asleep on it often enough. In the short term, it was fine, but how long would it be before they caught Zac? She really needed to find a better solution.

"You have next Friday afternoon booked out as well," Gauri said, clearly irritated at the extra burden she was placing on them all.

"That's for Gerry Brown's medical tribunal," Callie told her senior partner. "There's nothing I can do about that."

She was surprised to find that Miller was out when she got to the police station, but pleased to see that Jeffries was gone too.

"The DI should be back shortly," Jayne Hales told her. "Mind you, he's so grumpy today, I'd rather he stayed out."

"Sorry," Callie said. "I think that's my fault."

Jayne raised one eyebrow and gave her a quizzical look by way of reply.

"He kept watch outside my flat last night," she explained. "That's what I wanted to talk to him about."

"Aah, yes, he did look a little crumpled when he arrived this morning."

"He can't keep on doing it," Callie said.

"Doing what?" Jeffries asked, making her jump because she hadn't seen him come into the room.

"Sleeping outside my flat. In his car," she clarified, as she really didn't want him to get the idea that Miller had been inside her flat. Ever. His imagination would run riot.

"So do us all a favour and go away somewhere, anywhere, until we find that scrote Zac."

"Unfortunately, I have a job to do and it's here in Hastings. Just don't go and harass his mother, he's already said that he'd escalate things if you do that."

"Sounds like a plan then," he replied and went off in search of tea and biscuits, leaving Callie wishing she had never mentioned Zac's mother. She turned back to Jayne.

"I don't suppose you are any nearer to finding him, are you?"

"Not really, I'm afraid," Jayne replied. "There's been a lot of talk on the street about him picking up where he left off."

"He's back dealing drugs?"

"And he seems to have recruited a couple of girls again as well."

"He's been busy," Callie said.

"Oh yes, he has definitely been busy and he's told people he's after payback for you and Marcy putting him away for so long." Jayne gave Callie a long hard look, but Callie did her best not to react. "And it's not just you, a couple of low-level dealers are in hospital having been beaten up, but apparently they don't remember how it happened, let alone who did it, so you really do need to take this seriously."

"I know, believe me. But I'm sure he'll turn up sooner or later," Callie said, hoping that he wouldn't do anything else to upset her, or harm her, in the meantime. "What's happening about the bones?" she asked, changing the subject deftly.

"Two complete bodies. All bones excavated and removed. The CSI team are just checking the rest of the garden but it doesn't look like there are any more body parts anywhere, thank goodness."

"That's a relief. Are you any closer to identifying who the skeletons might belong to?" Callie asked.

"No," Jayne shook her head. "No one's been reported missing." She turned to DC Nigel Nugent. "Anything on previous house owners, Nigel?"

"I have a list from the council of all their tenants, and I have the land registry details of all the people who have owned it since it was sold." He held out a sheet of paper and Callie took it from him.

"It was first bought from the council in 1985 by a man called Derek Childs who had lived there for the previous twenty years. He sold it on to the owners before the current ones in 2010 and then it was bought by the Mitchells just over a year ago."

Callie looked at the paper he had given her, it said exactly what he had just told her.

"It was a Mr and Mrs Cooper who sold it to the Mitchells," Callie said. "Do we know any more about them?"

"Simon Cooper lives in Bexhill now; we've just been to see him. They sold up because they were getting divorced." Jeffries was back, mug of tea in his hand. Callie was relieved to find out that they hadn't been to see Zac's mother.

"And Mrs Cooper?" Jayne asked him. "Is she around?"

"He has had little contact with her since she took the kids and went back up north somewhere. The boss is getting the local force to check on their welfare."

"How old would the children be?" Callie asked, suddenly anxious.

"Eight and ten. Mr Cooper could at least remember that detail." Jayne looked at Callie and added, "The pathology report is in and it says that the skeletons were of an adult man and woman so at least we know it can't be the kids."

"And nothing to indicate cause of death?"

"The male had a hairline fracture of the skull that could be the COD."

"Anything else interesting?" Callie asked.

"Well." Jayne hesitated. "He did say that there were signs of considerable wear and tear of the joints and that the–" She paused and picked up a sheet of paper and handed it to Callie.

"The sphenotemporal and temporoparietal sutures were completely fused in both skeletons so he estimated their ages to be over seventy," she read out.

"Definitely not the children then," Jeffries conceded.

"And the woman? Anything to indicate COD there?" she asked.

"Nada. Best he could say is that there's no sign of nicks on the bones to suggest stabbing, no bullet holes, and they managed to find the hyoid bones for both corpses and they were intact."

Callie knew that made strangulation unlikely but not impossible, and certainly didn't rule out smothering or drugging as causes of death.

"I don't suppose there were any other findings to aid identification? Old broken bones? Hip replacements? Breast implants?"

"Nothing helpful at all. Not even teeth. They both must have worn full dentures." Jayne hesitated before adding, "And they didn't find them buried with the bodies, either."

"They must have had a dentist at some point, then. Is there any way of checking with local ones and seeing if they have any record of any of the previous owners or tenants with false teeth? I mean, every little pointer to us having the right people would help, wouldn't it?" Callie looked at Jayne and Jayne looked at Nigel.

"I'll add it to my list," he said, but he didn't sound happy. The list must be very long.

"What about soil analysis?" Callie asked. "For any signs of drugs in the earth around them?" It was a long shot, but if they had been killed with some kind of drug or poison, traces might theoretically still be found in the soil, provided it hadn't been washed away by the rain over the years.

"That will take months and there's little hope of finding anything after all this time either. There were fragments of cloth found with the female body, some kind of polyester that hadn't completely disintegrated, possibly from a nightdress, they thought. And a label, but they haven't been able to get anything readable from that yet. I think the DI is negotiating to have the money for further testing."

Callie knew that wasn't going to be easy. Budgets were a perennial problem and they couldn't yet show that a major crime had been committed.

"What about the man? Was he naked?" she asked.

"All they could find was a bit of cord by the male's waist, like a pyjama cord, possibly. But no buttons."

"So, they think that they were both buried in their nightwear?"

"It's tempting to think that, but it's not definite," Jayne told her firmly.

"Two, unidentified elderly people, someone must know who they are. Someone must have missed them, surely?" Callie asked but she wasn't expecting a reply.

"I don't suppose Mr Cooper admitted to having buried anyone in the garden?" Jayne asked Jeffries.

"Unfortunately, not," he told her. "In fact, he seemed as surprised about it as the Mitchells were."

"And did he know the previous owner?" Callie looked down at her list. "Derek Childs?"

"Never met him, apparently. It was all done through Puttocks, the estate agents, and yes, we'll be going to see them shortly," Jeffries told her. "Soon as the boss– ah, here he is." Jeffries looked at the door as Steve Miller walked in, looking as immaculate as usual.

"Soon as I do what?" Miller asked him testily.

"Soon as you finish talking to the plods up north, boss, checking on the welfare of the Cooper family."

"Who? Ah yes," Miller looked momentarily confused before catching on to his sergeant's meaning, making Callie wonder what he had really been up to. She could see from the expression on Jayne's face that she was wondering too. "The Coopers, yes. They're going to go around and see them straight away and will let us know."

"So now we're going to the estate agents who dealt with the sale, aren't we?" Jeffries took a final slurp of tea before depositing his mug on Jayne's desk. "Best get onto it straight away."

"Absolutely, yes." Miller turned to Callie. "Nothing's happened, has it?"

"No, but…" She dropped her voice, not wanting the entire room to hear what she said even though it was clear that they were all listening intently. "You can't sleep outside my flat every night. You will exhaust yourself."

"I need to know you are safe," he replied, as quietly as she had.

"Why don't you just invite him to share your bed," Jeffries chipped in, loudly. "That way he can really be sure."

Miller threw him a filthy look as everyone else in the room looked intently at their computer screens. Callie could feel a red flush rising up her neck, any moment now her cheeks would be bright red so she was pleased when Miller decided that discretion was the better part of valour and left the incident room with Jeffries in tow, the latter grinning with delight at having embarrassed them both.

Callie took a deep breath and tried to ignore the twinkle in Jayne's eye.

"Have you got the archaeology or anthropology reports back from the university yet?" she asked Jayne in order to distract her.

"No, not yet. Could be weeks," Jayne replied. "I don't suppose any of the previous owners are patients of yours?"

"The names don't ring a bell,' Callie replied, "but it's quite likely. Derek Childs would have been before my time, of course, but Linda might remember him, or Hugh. I'll ask them."

Linda, the practice manager, had been at the practice for almost twenty years, in one role or another, but Hugh Grantham had been there from when the practice first opened. Retired now, and looking after his terminally ill wife, he had a reputation for never forgetting a patient. He was dearly loved by the local community and couldn't walk down the street without someone stopping to talk to him. He always managed to remember to ask after partners or children, and what they were up to and how they were. Callie had no idea how he could recall details like that. If anyone would remember Derek Childs, it would be Hugh.

Chapter 11

"Do you remember a patient called Derek Childs?" Callie asked Linda before going downstairs to do her evening clinic.

"Can't say that I do," Linda replied and a quick search of the system didn't bring up any patients by that name.

"He must predate us going computerised," Linda said.

It would be hard to find a patient from so long ago. His paper records would have been returned to the family practitioner committee when he left, or died, and he would have been removed from his doctor's list. Dr Grantham was her last hope of finding out and between patients, Callie called him and arranged to visit. Then she rang Kate to let her know that she wouldn't need an escort home. She promised to do the short trip, there and back, by taxi.

"I'll see you at home, then. Bye!" Callie said, quickly cutting off any protest her friend might make.

As she put the phone down, she buzzed for her final patient of the evening to come in. Fortunately, it was an easy matter to resolve and she was soon finished.

Pulling on her coat, she grabbed her bag and headed for the door. She could see the taxi waiting at the kerb for her, ignoring the impatient toots of cars trying to pass. She came out of the surgery and heard the door click shut behind her. At this time of night, when all the clinics had finished and only staff remained, the door was on automatic lock and there was no one at the reception desk. The few remaining staff were in the office upstairs, or checking doors and windows prior to setting the alarm and the main door locks and going home themselves.

As she exited the building, she suddenly realised that someone was standing, slightly to the side of the main entrance. As she came out, he began moving quickly towards her.

Heart racing, Callie made a split-second decision. She would need to get her keys out and unlock the door if she chose to try and get back into the safety of her workplace. It would take too long, so she ran for the waiting taxi.

"Callie!" the person called out as she opened the taxi door and flung herself into the car. He grabbed at her arm and she dropped her handbag, which spilled open, scattering her purse, pens and keys on the ground. She leant down to grab her things and the man who had called out to her, bent down to help. He was wearing a dark jacket, baseball cap, and had a scarf around the lower part of his face, so, for a single terrifying moment, she didn't recognise him. It was only as he looked up when she saw to her relief that it was Gerry Brown who had been waiting for her, not Zac or one of his thugs. He still had her handbag and keys in his hand and dropping the keys into the bag, held it out for her to put the rest of her things back in it.

"Callie!" he said. "We need to talk."

"No, we shouldn't do that. We are not supposed to have any contact, Gerry, you know that. Not before the hearing," she told him through the still open door of the taxi. "And you need to stay away from Hastings, and me. You know what Mr Hemsworth will do if he catches you here."

"I know, but I need you to understand–"

"No!" she said firmly and slammed the door shut. "Let's go." She told the driver where she was going as he pulled away, causing another car to stop suddenly as it was trying to pass. Looking back, she could see Gerry still standing in the middle of the road, looking lost.

* * *

Dr Hugh Grantham's home in St Leonards was a 19th century lodge that formed part of the gatehouse at the top of Maze Hill, a lovely park that Callie had often taken strolls with Dr Grantham in when he was a senior partner and she was a very new doctor in his practice.

"Come in, come in," he said with a smile when he opened the door. Callie waved to the taxi driver who was kindly waiting to make sure she got safely into the house, and followed Dr Grantham into the light and bright sitting room. Hugh's wife Esme was on a chaise longue by the window, and looked up as Callie came into the room.

"Callie, how lovely to see you." Esme held out a hand as Callie walked over to her and took it gently. It didn't take a doctor to know that Esme was ill, or that she needed to be handled with care. She was very pale, with deep, dark bags under her eyes, and the paper-thin skin on her hand had been bruised and marked by every slight knock.

"How are you, Esme?" Callie asked.

"Oh, I'm as well as can be expected," Esme replied with a small smile. "So long as you don't expect too much." Despite the ravages that her terminal illness, and the side effects of the medications they were using to try and slow down the progression of the cancer that was eating her body, Esme was still beautiful. "I hear you want to quiz Hugh about one of his patients?"

"Well, I'm trying to find out if this man ever was one. Linda hasn't been able to help, so–"

"If he was ever a patient, Hugh will remember him," Esme said proudly and turned to her husband who was hovering protectively at her side. "Take her into your study, Hugh, and I'll just have a little rest." The effort of speaking did seem to have left her a bit breathless.

"You'll ring if you need anything?" Hugh asked her and made sure that the antique side table was close by, so that she could reach her book, drink and the small silver bell for her to summon him if she needed help.

"Of course," Esme said and turned back to Callie. "Tell him not to fuss so, won't you?" She then lay back and closed her eyes.

"Of course," Callie said quietly and then followed Hugh out into the hall and through to his study.

He sat at his desk in the room Callie knew so well. It was exactly the study she would have designed for an elderly doctor: a large mahogany desk, the book-lined walls and original watercolours on the wall, paintings she knew had been done by Hugh Grantham himself, art having been the second love of his life, or perhaps third. Esme, his patients and then art, she thought was the correct order. She wondered what he would do with himself once Esme died. Would he want to come back to work? She thought not. She hoped he would be able to fill his time with art and that it would be enough. But she had her doubts.

"Now, what's this patient's name and why do you need to know about him?" Hugh asked her, breaking her chain of thought.

"It's a bit of a long story," she said and went on to tell it.

* * *

Callie called Kate as she left Dr Grantham's home to let her know that she was on her way back and was surprised when the call went straight through to the answerphone. Perhaps she was in the loo, or had her phone on silent. Callie dismissed her fleeting anxiety and left a message.

"Hi, Kate, just to let you know I'm on my way back. I'll be home shortly, so let me know if you want me to pick up a takeaway or anything. Bye!"

Halfway back to her home, Callie heard the ping of a text-message and pulled out her phone again.

The message read: 'Don't come in. Stay in taxi. Text me and I'll join you.'

Callie smiled, and then frowned. Her first thought had been that Kate planned to go out for a meal, her second that something had happened.

Callie asked the taxi driver to toot his horn and wait as they pulled up outside her building and then got out of the cab and approached her front door cautiously.

It was immediately flung open by Kate who handed her two suitcases.

"What's going on?" Callie asked.

"I'll tell you later," Kate replied as she took Callie's arm and tried to guide her towards the waiting taxi.

"And what's that smell?" Callie stood her ground and wrinkled her nose. "It's like bleach mixed with–" She sniffed again.

"Dog shit," Kate said, grabbing one of the bags back and slamming the door shut behind her. Callie followed her towards the waiting taxi.

"Who on earth brought a dog home. Oh!" Callie stopped as she suddenly realised what must have happened. "Someone put dog poo through the letter box?"

"That's not very nice," the taxi driver said as he put the cases in the boot and settled them both in the car. "Was it that bloke earlier who jumped out at you?" he asked.

"He went to your work?" Kate gasped.

"No, that was just Gerry, he wanted to speak to me and was angry when I refused."

"Par for the course." Kate snorted.

"Thank you," Callie said after a few moments' thought.

"What for?" Kate asked.

"Cleaning it up," she said. "I'm guessing that was you wielding the bleach."

"Yes," Kate grimaced at the memory. "That was me, indeed. And remind me not to get a dog. God, it smelled vile."

"I bet it did. Did the neighbours realise what had happened?"

"Well, your neighbour in the middle—"

"Howard," Callie filled in for her.

"Yes, Howard, didn't notice it until he'd walked it all the way up to his front door and it seems that he doesn't keep any cleaning products in the house."

Callie could imagine that of her downstairs neighbour.

"And the old bat in the bottom flat—"

"Mrs Drysdale."

"Was far too busy telling me what to do to actually help."

"That sounds true to form, and I'm sorry I wasn't there to help."

"That's not the problem."

"No," Callie agreed as they arrived at Kate's house and the taxi driver got out to fetch their cases from the car boot.

"Seems to me you've upset quite a few people," he said as he handed them the cases.

"She can't help herself," Kate replied before Callie could. "It's her abrasive personality."

Despite herself, Callie was laughing as they went into the small fisherman's cottage where Kate lived.

"Abrasive personality? The cheek of it!"

"Well you have to admit that, as the cabbie said, you do seem to have upset an awful lot of people lately," Kate said, and Callie really couldn't argue with that. "Just ask Mrs Drysdale what she thinks of you as a neighbour."

"Oh, I think I know what she would have to say," Callie groaned. "She was pretty angry before, but now she's really not going to be happy with me."

"Understatement of the year," Kate said.

"Am I going to have to look for a new home?" Callie asked as she flopped into Kate's enormously squishy sofa, so much more comfortable than her own more elegant model.

"I don't think it's quite that bad but keeping your head down for a few weeks wouldn't be a bad idea. Wine?" Kate went off to the kitchen to find a bottle of wine and some glasses, leaving Callie to think about her situation.

When Kate returned, there was a knock at the door and Kate went to answer it, returning a few moments later with Steve Miller behind her. He wasn't looking happy.

"Sorry," Kate said. "I rang him as soon as I realised what had happened."

"That's okay, I would have called too, eventually," Callie replied.

"I've got patrols out looking for him, but nothing so far," Miller said as he sat down.

"What about video?" Callie asked, sitting forward as she suddenly thought of it. "From the doorbell?" She checked her pockets for her phone. "I should have thought of it earlier."

"We already have that," Kate said. "From, what's-his-name, How or Howard? Better on technology than cleaning."

"And?" She looked at them both.

"Definitely our Zac," Miller told her. "Looked straight at the camera and made a gesture as he put the, um, stuff through the letter box."

Callie sighed. It was all very well having the technology in place to keep her safe, but it didn't help if it just meant the criminals stuck two fingers up at it, or, in this case, probably only the one.

"Oh," she said, suddenly remembering her visit to Hugh Grantham. "Derek Childs. The man who owned the house with the bones before the Coopers or the Mitchells."

"Yes?" Miller leant forward, eager to hear her news.

"I spoke to Hugh. He was a patient, until about fifteen years ago," she told him. "Lived there with his wife, possibly called Deirdre, but he wasn't sure. They were both in their early seventies, Derek had angina and type two diabetes, but nothing imminently life threatening. Deirdre was showing early signs of dementia, although he said it was hard to be sure because she had never been that communicative, so when neither of them came into the surgery for a while, he knocked on the door when he was doing a visit nearby to see if they were okay."

"That was good of him," Kate said.

"Hugh was like that, a good old-fashioned GP, believed in looking out for his patients," Callie responded. "Anyway, it was Simon Cooper who answered the door, said he'd bought the house off Mr Childs. At the time, Cooper said he thought Mr Childs was going into an old people's home somewhere up north, to be closer to family. Hugh thought that was a bit odd as he didn't think there was any family left and that Derek was definitely a

Hastings man, born and bred. Cooper didn't seem to know anything else."

"I'll get Nigel onto tracking what happened to them both tomorrow," Miller said.

"Have you eaten?" Kate asked him.

"I'm meeting Bob. He's taken a couple of uniforms to raid an address where Zac's supposed to be staying. See if he's there. But he'd have rung if he'd been successful." Miller looked accusingly at his phone as if it was responsible for them not finding Zac.

"And what about earlier, what were you off doing?" Callie asked, remembering how shifty he and Jeffries had looked as they left.

"Ah, yes, well we went back to his mother's address, but…" He shrugged.

"Well that explains the dog poo. He did warn me he would do more if you harassed his mum." Callie tried not to sound irritated. "Let's hope that's enough for him and he doesn't decide to do something else." She knew she shouldn't blame Miller, someone had to check Zac hadn't gone back home, but he might have warned her he was going to do it.

Miller left soon after, having been assured that they were staying in for the night.

"I'll make sure there are plenty of patrols in case he comes here," he said as he went to leave.

"Just so long as you don't camp outside in your car overnight," Callie said to him.

"Not when there's a perfectly good sofa in here that you can sleep on," Kate added pointing to where Callie was sitting. Miller finally agreed that when he came back later, he would sleep downstairs.

"We'll just have to hope Bob Jeffries doesn't get to hear about it," Callie said once he had gone. "You can imagine what he would say if he knew Steve was spending the night with me, even if it is in a different room."

"What does it matter what he says?" Kate asked her. "You are both grown-ups, after all."

But that didn't stop Callie from worrying about it.

"The only reason I'm agreeing to it at all is because I feel bad enough about putting you in danger and if having him sleep on your sofa is the price I have to pay to ensure your safety, then that's what it will have to be."

"You need to stop worrying about other people and think about yourself for once," Kate told her firmly. "Are you hungry? I've got a frozen pizza I can offer you, and I even have a bit of salad you can have on the side if you want to be healthy."

"That sounds perfect. Shall I make the salad for us both?" Callie started to stand up.

"Absolutely not," Kate replied. "No salad for me, thank you. I have mozzarella sticks and garlic dough balls to go with mine and if you're good, I might even let you have one or two of those as well. Now sit down and pour yourself another glass of wine."

As Callie sat back and did as she had been ordered, she thought how amazing it was to have such good friends as Kate and Steve, and how she would hate to have to start all over again, making new friends in a new place. Home is where your heart is, she thought. But Belfast would never feel like home to her, even with Billy there; home, to her, was where your friends were.

Chapter 12

It wasn't until lunchtime the next day, when Callie was sitting in the office with a cup of instant coffee and a rather rubbery cheese salad sandwich that Linda had bought for her, that she got a phone call from Nigel at the police station.

"I've got Derek and Deirdre Childs' birth certificates but after that it's a blank," he said. "No passports ever issued, so it's unlikely they went abroad and there's no record of death certificates for either of them. All the care homes I've called have denied ever having them in residence. Of course, I've hardly made a dent in the list as we don't know where they went. I started with local ones but even doing that, I've got a lot more to contact. It will take weeks, if not months." He sounded understandably dispirited.

"I know, I wish I could help narrow things down a bit."

"It's not your fault, and I'm sure we will find them if they are in a care home but I can't believe they are both still alive. Derek would be ninety-four and Deirdre was older. She'd be ninety-eight according to her birth certificate."

"Maybe they both came from particularly long-lived families," Callie said, although her tone revealed the doubts she had.

"But you told the DI that Derek had heart disease and diabetes and Deirdre was already showing signs of dementia when Dr Grantham last saw them, didn't you?"

"That's right," she said. "It does seem unlikely that they are still alive, but you never know, they could be sitting quietly in a home somewhere." Or they could have been buried in their back garden. Callie had to admit the possibility to herself and she heard Nigel sigh. "What about their pensions? Do we know what address the DWP have?"

"We're waiting on the warrant. They are very hot on data protection at the DWP, but hopefully we'll get it eventually." Despite his words, he didn't sound hopeful.

"But what about mail from the pension people? They send out letters about fuel payments and things, don't they? Has anyone said they got any letters?"

Callie heard Nigel sigh before he answered.

"Mr Cooper said they might have, but they would have chucked them in the bin. The Mitchells say they haven't had any that they remember."

Callie joined in with the sighing. It all seemed pretty hopeless.

"What does Steve think about you calling round care homes?" she asked him.

"That there are probably better ways of spending my time. After all, this could just be a case of failing to report a death and preventing lawful burial."

"I take your point, but two of them? Buried together? I can't help feeling that these deaths have to be suspicious."

"I know, I know, but after all this time, what hope do we have of proving anything?"

Callie knew that Steve would have to fight for funds for the investigation unless there was some concrete evidence of serious crime.

I'd best get back to trying to contact every care home in the country," Nigel told her.

She could tell he wasn't looking forward to the job and would be delighted if a displacement activity came along. Any displacement activity at all, other than calling dentists.

"Is the DI there?" she asked.

"No, he's out with DS Jeffries."

Callie suspected that they were both out trying to find Zac Tindall and she felt guilty that so much of their time was being taken up by trying to protect her; but at the same time, she was extremely grateful. She just hoped they found him soon. Then the only question would be if she could ever move back into her flat. She was pretty sure she could talk Howard in the middle flat round, but Mrs Drysdale was a different matter altogether.

* * *

"You think the bodies are this old couple then?" Kate asked her later. "Derek and Deirdre Childs?"

"Looks likely, doesn't it? I mean, they would be very old if they were still alive. And if they aren't still breathing, being buried in the back garden would explain the lack of death certificates."

"Yes, but the real question is how did they get there? I mean, they can hardly have buried themselves."

"Quite."

It was, indeed, the real question Callie thought, as there was a knock at the door.

"It's probably Steve," Callie said as Kate got up to see who was there. Callie quickly checked how she looked in the mirror, though hating herself for doing so. Her hair was as perfect as always, but her mascara had smudged very slightly. She licked a finger to wipe the worst of it away and was suddenly aware of a commotion at the door and rushed into the hall to see what was going on.

Kate was standing at the door which was partially open and prevented from opening further by the security chain which she had sensibly engaged before answering the door.

"No! you cannot come in to speak to her," Kate was saying.

"Just for a moment, please!" A man's voice replied, urgently. Callie recognised it as belonging to Gerry Brown. "It really is a matter of life and death."

"It's okay," Callie said, putting a restraining hand on Kate's arm, stopping her from slamming the door in his face. "I'll speak to him."

"Are you sure?" Kate queried, but seeing that Callie was determined, she stood back and let her friend take her place and speak through the small gap.

"I'm not letting you in, Gerry," she told him firmly. "And you better keep it quiet and respectful or I will shut the door."

"Fine, that's fine," Gerry replied, but he sounded unhappy with this request. "I just hoped that we could sit down and discuss this in a reasonable manner."

"Not going to happen," Kate said loudly from behind Callie.

"We could go to the pub," he offered. "Away from…"

Kate and Gerry had been out together at one point, and he had stalked her when she decided to call it off, until she threatened him with legal action.

"Not going to happen," Kate repeated, more loudly, from the hall.

"I can't, Gerry. There are… other things going on, so I really can't go out. Now, what is it you want to discuss?"

"Look, as I've tried to tell you, I'm a changed man, I'm having therapy."

There was a snort from Kate at this point, letting him know what she thought of that, and also telling him that she was still listening to what he had to say.

"Look, this is difficult with…" He gestured towards Kate within the house.

"I know, but it is what it is, so get on with it before I lose patience." Callie wasn't going to give way – Kate would never forgive her.

"I just want you to give me a second chance," he finally said.

"Second?" Callie queried. "You've had a lot more chances than that, Gerry. And stuffed them up every time."

"I know, but honestly it won't happen again."

"Why? What's different this time?"

"I really am having therapy and I know I won't get any more chances. I have to get myself sorted out."

"Gerry, you slept with a patient, and not for the first time, I might add. I can't turn a blind eye to that and even if I did, I'm not the only one giving evidence."

"I know, but if you don't support what Jessica says, I can convince them it didn't happen, I'm sure I can, because it didn't."

"I have to support my patient, Gerry, you know that. It wouldn't be fair for me to withdraw now, even if I wanted to, which I don't."

"But she made it up," he said in desperation. "I'm sure I can convince the board of that. And anyway, she might not even be there."

"What makes you say that?" Callie, asked, her suspicions immediately raised.

Gerry realised that perhaps he had said too much.

"She's flaky as hell, you know that. I know I'm not supposed to have any contact with her, and I haven't, all right?"

"And if you believe that, you'll believe anything," Kate said.

"Shut up! This has nothing to do with you." Gerry leant on the door and thumped it in frustration. Callie tried to close it against him but he was too strong and she wasn't sure how much more the thin security chain would hold. Or the doorframe for that matter. There was the screech of a car stopping.

"Oi! What's going on here?"

Callie was sure the voice belonged to Jeffries, and she sighed with relief.

The weight came off the door and Callie was able to close it as Gerry was hauled back by Jeffries. She leant against the closed door and took a deep breath. Outside she could hear Bob Jeffries having very blunt words with Gerry.

"Don't you fucking tell me to leave you alone," he was saying. "You may or may not have the right to be here in a public place, but she has every right to tell you to sling your hook and if you don't, I have every fucking right to arrest you. Is that clear?"

Callie hurried into the small living room so that she could look through the window and see what was happening outside. Kate had beaten her to it.

"I think Bob is a little bit angry," Kate said with a grin.

Looking out, Callie could see that Jeffries' car was blocking the street, driver's door still open. It looked as if he had been going past and seen Gerry thumping on the door, and had stopped and jumped out to confront him. Jeffries had hold of Gerry Brown's collar and had pushed him up against the car.

"I'd better go out before he's beaten to a pulp," Callie said.

"It's no more than he deserves," Kate responded, but her heart wasn't in it. "Oh, all right. I suppose it's for the best," she conceded. "Don't want Bob to get into trouble over a waste of space like Gerry Brown."

They both went to the front door, and, undoing the security chain, went out into the street.

Kate's street was very narrow, with parking on one side only and just about enough room to turn around at the dead end where there were steps down to Rock-a-Nore where Callie worked.

"Did Zac Tindall tell you to come here?" Bob was shouting at a completely bewildered Gerry.

"It's okay, Bob," Callie said as she approached Jeffries' car. "He's got nothing to do with Zac."

Jeffries seemed reluctant to let his prisoner go. "You sure?"

"And Gerry," Callie said. "I've told you before, you need to leave Hastings."

"Don't worry," Gerry replied. "I have, I just want to talk to you."

A car pulled up behind Bob Jeffries' car and the driver wound his window down.

"What's going on?" he asked.

"Police," Jeffries told him. "Now back up and find somewhere else to park, mate."

The driver looked as if he might argue, but eventually began to back up the road.

"Perhaps you'd like to tell me why you were trying to force your way into that house?" Jeffries still had hold of Gerry by his jacket lapels.

"I just wanted to speak to her and I'm very sorry, I got a bit frustrated when she wouldn't let me in."

"Yeah? Well you need to learn when to take a hint, mate."

Jeffries didn't know that he had hit the nail on the head. That had always been Gerry's problem: knowing when he wasn't wanted.

"And it's not going to persuade me out of giving evidence at the hearing either, Gerry," Callie told him.

"It would make me even more determined," Kate chipped in and then they all turned as they heard a shout and the frantic footsteps of someone running towards them from the cliff steps. It was Miller.

"What's going on?" he said as soon as he was close enough.

"Good question," Jeffries answered.

* * *

It had taken more than half an hour for Callie to explain everything again and for Gerry to be sent off home with a flea in his ear and a warning not to go anywhere near Callie or Kate again. He seemed to have finally understood that getting arrested for harassment wouldn't help his case.

"How did he know where you were staying?" Miller asked.

"He knows Kate and I are close, if I wasn't at home the odds are I would be here," she told him.

"I'm amazed he had the nerve," Kate said. "After what happened when we split up." It was a fair point.

"I need to find out if he has put pressure on Jessica to drop her evidence," Callie said.

"I'd put money on him doing exactly that," Kate agreed. "That man really makes me angry. How I ever went out with him, I'll never know."

"Don't be so hard on yourself," Callie told her. "You didn't really know him then and you only saw him a couple of times, didn't you?"

"Yes, but I should be able to spot the scary ones earlier than that."

Realising that everyone was going to be around for quite a long time, Kate had sent out for enough curry and side dishes to feed an army. They were now sitting in the living room, eating from plates on their laps because Kate's dining table wasn't big enough for four.

"He sounds a right slimeball," Jeffries said when Callie had finished telling them about Gerry's many problems and his current one with the suspension and hearing. "I remember him now from when we had him in for questioning over those murders – you know, the ones where the killer was picking his victims from that website?"

Callie could indeed remember the case. It was when she had first met Gerry, because he was doing a locum job in her surgery, having been allowed to work again after his first term of suspension.

"Anyway, the good news is we have a lead on where Zac might have been hiding out," Miller said between mouthfuls of keema naan. "We got reports about a flat being taken over by drug dealers."

"Cuckooing?" Jeffries asked. Both Callie and Kate had no need to ask for an explanation; they had both dealt with similar cases where someone elderly or vulnerable was befriended by a drug dealer who then moved in and essentially took over their flat. It could be a very frightening experience for the flat owner – or renter – as they were usually threatened with violence if they resisted or tried to go to the police.

"Yes," Miller agreed. "It was raided this morning. A bunch of people were arrested and they found a large quantity of Class A drugs there as well."

"And Zac was among the arrestees?" Callie asked hopefully.

"No, but I got news earlier that some things belonging to Zac had been found there when they searched the place. All the suspects will be re-interviewed tomorrow and asked about him. See if they know where he's gone."

"Something to look forward to," Jeffries said, trying in vain to catch a dribble of curry sauce before it hit his tie.

* * *

I really want to do something bad to her, to punish her, but I can't, not yet. There's no chance to get to her with that bitch and the police watching her like a hawk, but they can't keep it up forever. They will go to their homes and she will let her guard down eventually, and when she does, I will know exactly where to find her.

Chapter 13

Kate was unusually grumpy as she walked Callie to work the next morning.

"Why do you have to start work this bloody early?" she moaned as they went down the steps together.

Callie, who had been up for quite a while and had had time to have breakfast, two cups of tea and a chat with Billy before her friend had even appeared, bleary eyed and craving coffee, wasn't sympathetic.

"To fit patient appointments in before they need to start work, and anyway, think of all the paperwork you'll be able to get done before you start getting interruptions."

"Hmph," was Kate's only reply to that.

At the bottom of the steps, Kate waited while Callie walked on to the surgery, only turning to head for her office once she was sure Callie was safely inside.

Callie smiled to herself as she went up the stairs to the office. She was under no illusions – there was little chance that her friend was going into the office at this hour. Kate would stop for breakfast at one of the many cafés she would pass on her way there.

Later, when she was taking a coffee break between calling patients, Gauri Sinha, came in.

"Do you have time for a quick word?" Gauri asked her.

"Of course." Callie sloshed some milk into her mug and followed Gauri into the doctors' office. It was empty at this time of the morning as most of the team did their paperwork at the end of their morning surgeries.

"I have had a complaint," Gauri said without preamble.

"Oh? From Mr Herring again? I did apologise for running late but you know what he's like once he–"

"No," Gauri interrupted her. "The GMC."

"What!" Callie was astounded. "What on earth is that about?"

"Have a seat, Callie," Gauri said and Callie did. She was genuinely taken aback to know that someone had made a formal complaint against her.

"It seems that Dr Brown has reported you for having contact with him prior to the hearing."

It took Callie a few moments to process this.

"This is absolute rubbish! He approached me. Repeatedly. Accosted me outside the surgery and came to my door last night – well, Kate's door – demanding to be let in."

"That's as may be, but they have taken his complaint seriously and have stopped proceedings against Dr Brown while they investigate. They are sending a lawyer down to speak to you."

"I have witnesses, Gauri. He was the one harassing me. In fact, the police were there last night and sent him off with a warning."

"That's good. I suggest you think about your contacts with him and who can verify them and present it all when the lawyer comes at two o'clock. Meanwhile, there is no question of you being suspended or anything. It's only the case against Dr Brown that is affected, so I suggest you go and see your patients, and try not worry about it."

Fat chance of that, Callie thought as she hurried back down to her consulting room. Gerry Brown had wasted no time in putting in his complaint. He must have rung them first thing for all this to have been arranged so quickly. She looked at the long list of patients she still had to call back and who would be anxiously waiting by their phones. They would have to wait a little longer, she decided reluctantly. Her first job was to call Kate and get her perspective. Callie suspected that she would insist on being present when the GMC lawyer interviewed her at two o'clock, at least, she hoped so.

* * *

Unable to concentrate on repeat prescriptions and test results, Callie took a taxi to the police station as soon as she had finished with her morning list. Kate had been suitably aghast when she heard about the move by Gerry Brown and was busy reorganising her own schedule of appointments so that she could be at the surgery for the interview.

"If I'm running late," Kate said, "make him wait, or get him some coffee, pour it over him and insist on cleaning him up, I don't care what you do, but don't start the interview until I'm there."

At the police station they were also amazed that Dr Brown had turned the tables in that way.

"He's got a nerve," Jayne told her.

"He's just trying to stall things, because he knows he's going to be struck off this time," Callie explained.

"But why? The hearing's going to happen sometime or other and he's suspended meanwhile, so why bother delaying things?"

"Maybe he thinks it will give him more time to change my patient's mind about giving evidence, and to wear me down, as well."

"Bloody cheek."

"I agree," she said. "Do you have the final report on the bones?"

"Yes," Jayne turned and picked up a printout of the report. "Two adults, one male, one female, almost certainly over seventy. Nothing we didn't already know."

Callie flipped through the report.

"What about the teeth?" she asked. "Or rather the lack of them?"

"Nada," Jayne told her. "None in either skull or found at the burial site either."

"Which would fit with them having taken them out for the night."

"Exactly," Jayne said. "Both of them, all ready for bed, and then something fatal happens. Let's hope they died in their sleep."

Leaving Callie looking at the report, she went back to her own desk.

"Erm, Dr Hughes?" Nigel asked tentatively. "Can I ask you a question, as you're here."

"Of course, Nigel, what can I do for you?"

"Well, I haven't found any trace of Mr or Mrs Childs anywhere. But I have been through all the house-to-house reports and one of the neighbours, a Mrs Violet Osborne, said she never believed they went into a home and said something about it not being them that bought the house really, because they didn't have the money."

"Has anyone followed that up?" Callie asked, suddenly interested.

"Well, we weren't sure at that point who the bodies were, but now it looks likely that it's them until proven otherwise so I thought I'd go back and ask about it but she wasn't there."

"Out, or moved out?"

"Moved out after a fall. Temporarily, I think, although another neighbour wasn't sure that she would ever be fit to come back."

"Do you know where she's gone?"

"A care home, but…" He looked round, careful that no one could overhear and then continued in a whisper. "I can't go there, it's where my nan died. I, well, I complained to the manager there and things got a bit heated."

Callie couldn't really imagine Nigel losing his temper, but if he was going to, it might well be because he didn't think someone was looking after his grandmother as well as they should.

"I can't face that woman again, I really can't and I don't know what to tell the boss. I mean, he'll just tell me to man up or something."

Callie smiled her understanding. She knew that Nigel had been very attached to his nan and that her death had been devastating for him.

"That's okay, Nigel, I understand. Why don't you send me the details and I'll pop in and see this Mrs Osborne?" She checked her watch. "Might not be until tomorrow though, I've got a meeting I need to get back to."

He beamed at her. "That's fine, and thank you, Dr Hughes."

Callie thought about Violet Osborne all the way back to the surgery. She was pretty sure she was registered at the practice, although she wasn't sure she had ever actually met her. Given the location of the row of houses where the bones had been found, it was a good bet that most of the residents were registered with them. It was the closest surgery, and would have been even closer when they were in their old premises. She might just have time to run a search on addresses and see who amongst the people who lived there, both now and previously, she might know, or, at least, have a legitimate excuse to speak to and ask about Mr and Mrs Childs.

As the taxi stopped at some traffic lights, she looked out of the window and saw the mouse of a woman who had been outside the house when the bones were dug up. The one who seemed to have been with Brian Stenning. The woman was scurrying along the pavement, clutching her over-large handbag and looking nervously around her as she went. Callie wondered why she looked so anxious all the time, but the lights changed and the taxi pulled away and she turned her mind to the interview that was about to take place and the anger she still felt against Gerry bloody Brown. She needed to talk to Jessica, even if her father didn't want her to contact the girl. She had to make sure that Gerry Brown hadn't spoken to her or tried to get her to change her story.

Chapter 14

Callie had booked the small office for her meeting with the GMC lawyer and was making coffee for the tall, black, shaven-headed man who had already charmed the receptionist and Linda. Callie had had to insist she could manage to make him some coffee without help, just to get Linda to leave them alone. She was showing him into the meeting room when Kate arrived, out of breath and apologising for being late.

"Not at all, I'm so pleased to meet you. My name's Samuel Okojie," the lawyer said, holding out his hand and smiling. "Please call me Samuel."

Kate took his hand and held it for just a moment too long. Callie had seen her react like this to men before, particularly men as handsome and charming as Samuel. Callie gave her friend a quizzical look from behind the lawyer and was gratified to see Kate look slightly embarrassed and let go of his hand.

Once they were settled with their coffees, Samuel took out a new pad of paper and a fountain pen and addressed Kate.

"I was just saying to Dr Hughes, that this is merely an informal chat to discover what has been going on. As you are no doubt aware, Dr Brown has contacted us to say that Dr Hughes has been trying to speak to him about the hearing that was scheduled for next week."

"Has that been cancelled then?" Callie asked, trying to get him to speak to her rather than Kate. He seemed as taken with her friend as she was with him.

"Postponed, until this is cleared up," he replied briefly before turning back to Kate.

"Which is, of course, exactly what Dr Brown wants," Kate told him.

"What makes you think that?" he replied. "After all, he is suspended already, so it isn't as though he can practice medicine while he waits for the hearing."

"No, but he can still tell people, women he is trying to impress, that is, that he is a doctor," she replied without letting him know quite how she knew all about Gerry Brown's chat-up techniques.

"And you think that being struck off will stop him from doing that?"

He had a good point and both Callie and Kate had to acknowledge it. Samuel picked up his pen and pad and readied himself to take notes, finally turning to Callie.

"Perhaps you could tell me about when he has contacted you, as precisely as you can, and also list everyone who can confirm what happened each of those times?" he said to Callie.

"Well, he has tried ringing me several times. Linda, the practice manager can tell you if he has rung here, but it may take some time to be able to give you the exact dates and times. We get a lot of calls." She smiled ruefully and he nodded that he understood. Callie then fished out her phone and went through her own call log, showing Samuel the screen. "You can see here that they are all him calling me, not vice versa."

Samuel very carefully made a note of each call and the time and the fact that they were incoming calls rather than outgoing.

"And you have answered some of those. Can you tell me what was said?" he asked her.

"He was just asking me not to go to the hearing, telling me he hadn't done it, that I was ruining his life. And then he sent an email" – she brought it up on the screen – "here, threatening to kill himself if I went ahead with my support of Jessica's statement."

"I see." Samuel wrote all this down. "And he also confronted you at home?"

"Yes, and also here, at work," Callie told him. "He came here and waited outside until I came out. Fortunately, I had a taxi waiting to take me to a meeting, but he tried to stop me leaving."

"Did he physically try to stop you?"

"No, I thought he might, so I jumped in the taxi and told the driver to go. I am sure the driver will tell you about it."

"If needs be, I'll get his details from you. Were there any other witnesses on that occasion?"

"Other than the taxi driver?" Callie thought for a moment. "Not that I remember."

"And what about when he came to your house?"

"It was Kate's house, actually," Callie told him, and went on to describe the incident there, and the involvement of the police.

"I can confirm all of that," Kate told him when she had finished. "And I am quite willing to make a statement or give evidence if needed."

"Thank you," he said. "I don't think that will be necessary." He cleared his throat and looked intently at Kate. He seemed a little anxious about his next question. "I don't want to pry, but I understand you know Dr Brown from a… um, previous relationship?"

Callie was surprised to see her friend left slightly off-balance by this question.

"Yes," Kate replied and paused, thinking about how to explain her previous problems with Gerry Brown. "I went out with him a couple of times but then decided we weren't suited but he disagreed. He wouldn't take no for an answer, kept calling me and texting me and I ended up having to threaten him with legal action to stop him from further contact."

Samuel meticulously wrote all this down.

"Can I ask how you know about that?" Kate asked him.

"It's all in Dr Brown's statement," he told her.

"I assume he told you that I was biased against him and persuaded the patient to make a complaint for some reason, did he?"

"Something like that," Samuel told her gently. "But that doesn't necessarily mean that I, we, believe him. We just need to be sure we have investigated everything."

"And what did he say about the policemen who attended last night?" Callie asked, beginning to realise exactly what Dr Brown was saying about them both.

"That you are involved with one of them and that they would lie for you too," he admitted, and Callie could see exactly what defence Gerry Brown was going to use at the hearing: that Jessica had made up the affair and that she and Kate had helped her concoct the whole story to get their revenge on him.

"He is such a… such a…"

"Two-faced, lying, manipulative bastard?" Kate finished for her.

"Yes, that," Callie said. "And more."

* * *

After they had finished giving their statements, Callie and Kate showed Samuel out. Callie could have done it on her own, but Kate was keen to stay close. He solemnly shook hands with them both and gave Kate his card in case she wanted to clarify anything. Callie wasn't sure, but she thought that he might have winked when he said that. Kate scrabbled in her bag for one of her cards to give him, and definitely winked as she did so. Standing behind Samuel, Callie rolled her eyes.

"What are you like!" she said to her friend once the GMC lawyer was out of earshot, but Kate just grinned.

* * *

After work, Callie called for a taxi to take her back to her own home, just for a visit. She had warned Kate that she would be late and promised her to make sure the taxi stayed whilst she spoke to her neighbours and apologised to them for the dog poo incident. It would be expensive, but worth it, she knew.

Howard was predictably okay about it, happy to have the whisky and promising to let her know if he saw anyone hanging around.

"Not that I'm expecting there to be anyone, of course," Callie reassured him. He just gave a small smile in reply which said it all really. It wasn't the first time someone had targeted her at the flat, and he clearly suspected that it wouldn't be the last.

Mrs Drysdale was a different matter entirely. There was no way she was going to be mollified by the best bunch of flowers Callie could find in M&S.

"It's not just yourself you put at risk, it's all of us," she had told Callie, and it was a fair point. "My son's not happy, not happy at all. He thinks I should sell up and move somewhere safer."

"I'm very sorry, Mrs Drysdale, I honestly didn't mean to cause you any trouble and I promise, I won't be moving back in until I am quite sure that the man responsible is safely in jail."

"That's as maybe, but what about when he gets out again? Or someone else takes a dislike to you? I'll be talking to the estate agents in the morning," she said.

* * *

Later, after a shared Chinese takeaway with Kate, during which Kate never stopped talking about Samuel Okojie, Callie went upstairs for a shower and to call Billy. It wasn't long before she came down again with a frown on her face.

"That was a quick chat with Billy. Normally you spend hours billing and cooing at each other," Kate commented shrewdly.

"He was busy," Callie said as she took her empty mug into the kitchen and washed it up. "And tired," she added when she came back into the living room. She gave the wine bottle a shrewd look and sat down on the sofa. By the amount of wine left in the bottle, she reckoned that the call had given Kate time to pour herself at least one glass more.

Billy had been suitably angry that Gerry Brown was manipulating the story, but other than that he had shown little interest and had seemed almost in a rush to put the phone down.

"I hope they find this Zac person soon," Kate said. "I'm not saying it hasn't been lovely having you staying with me, but it will be nice not to have Miller sleeping on my couch."

"It is good of him to do that, though," Callie said.

"Bet he wouldn't do it for anyone else."

"I'm sure he would do it for any of his friends," Callie replied.

"Rubbish!" Kate rejoined. "We all know he's sweet on you."

Callie laughed. "Sweet on me? That's a very coy phrase for you."

"Well, got the hots for you, then."

"And it's not true anyway." Callie couldn't help a slight blush or the feeling of smug satisfaction that it gave her, even if she wasn't about to admit it.

"How did it go with your peacekeeping mission with your neighbours?" Kate asked and Callie grimaced by way of a reply.

"Not begging you to come home, then?" Kate laughed.

"Er, no, not Mrs Drysdale anyway and I felt very guilty," Callie told Kate. "I mean, if it was my mother, I'm not sure I'd be happy for her to live there alone after all that's happened."

"If it was your mother, no self-respecting criminal would dare come near," Kate replied, bringing a smile back to her friend's face.

"That's so very true," she said.

Chapter 15

It wasn't until lunchtime the next day that Callie was able to visit Mrs Violet Osborne, the old lady who had been a neighbour of Derek and Deirdre Childs that Nigel had asked her to interview for him. A brief check of her patient notes had revealed that she was indeed in a care home up on The Ridgeway, having had a fall that resulted in a sprained ankle, broken wrist and a couple of cracked ribs. Concerned that she couldn't really look after herself with her injuries, she had been admitted to a care home for a period of convalescence.

"I'm not staying here long, mind." She fixed Callie with a beady eye. "I'm not some doddery old dear to be left drooling in front of the telly. I will be going home as soon as I'm steady on my pins, so don't you go telling those namby-pamby social workers I'm not fit to look after myself."

"I wouldn't dream of it," Callie responded with a smile. "And anyway, I'm not here about you, well, not directly about you, Mrs Osborne." Callie was relieved that the old lady seemed in good spirits and, more importantly, of sound mind.

"Call me Violet, Mrs Osborne is much too formal," she insisted. "What are you here about then?"

"Do you remember Derek and Deirdre Childs?"

"Of course I do, there's nothing wrong with my memory. I lived next door to them for years. She was always, well, a bit simple, if you know what I mean. Probably not allowed to say that any more, but I'm too old to keep up with all that sort of thing."

"She had mild dementia, you mean?"

"Mild?" Violet snorted. "She was completely away with the fairies once that set in, but she'd always been a bit slow."

"And the dementia made it worse?"

"Couldn't be left on her own because she'd put the gas on and not light it, things like that. She was a danger to us all. That's why I'd go and sit with her sometimes when he needed to go out."

"You knew them both well?"

"Is that who the bones were? Was it her?"

"We don't know who the bones belonged to, yet." Callie wasn't sure whether or not to tell her that there were two skeletons just yet. "Why do you think it was her?"

"Because that husband of hers was up to something. I could tell."

"What makes you say that?"

"Because he always was up to something, I mean, where did he get the money to buy the house?"

"Mortgage?" Callie suggested.

"Who would give a mortgage to a man who wasn't working?"

"He was out of work?"

"Out more than in, had been all his life. Who was going to employ a man who was always complaining about his back or his heart or whatever else and was coming up for retirement age, anyway?"

"Perhaps he had an inheritance," Callie suggested.

"No one in that family ever had two pennies to rub together. No, he did something shifty to get the house, you mark my words. Then a few years later, they just upped and left."

"He didn't say they were going?"

"He'd been talking about going into that flash care home in Battle, you know, where you have your own flat and there's a warden to look after you. Boasting about what a lovely time they would have there. He said the house was going to be sold to pay for it."

Violet lay back against her pillows and closed her eyes, exhausted by the conversation. Her skin tone was only a shade or two darker than the crisp white pillows she rested on.

"I'm sorry, I've tired you out. I'll let you get some rest." Callie stood to leave, but Violet raised a hand to stop her.

"No, no, I just need to get my strength back. It's this place, makes you feel tired and I don't sleep so well here. All the comings and goings."

"I know, it's like being in hospital, they are the worst places for getting a rest."

"But I will be going back home soon. It's important when you're my age. I don't have a lot of time left and I want to die in my own bed, you understand?"

Callie patted her hand.

"Yes, yes I do," she said, and she did.

"Good, so maybe you'll help me get out of here, then? Payback for helping you with your questions. What do they call that? Something Latin."

"A quid pro quo," Callie answered with a laugh. "And yes, I will do my best to see that you get to go home as soon as possible. I'll contact social services. See about carers and whatever else we can do." Callie meant every word. She knew how short staffed the community and care services were, but she would do everything in her power to see to it that Violet was able to get home soon.

* * *

"Yes, yes, I do know just how difficult it is to find people willing to work as carers." Callie was getting nowhere. "But I really do need–" But the person on the other end had already hung up and she was so angry, she slammed the phone down.

"Careful," Linda said from the doorway. "I'll make you pay for a replacement if you break it."

"Sorry, I know there's no point in taking my frustration out on an inanimate object."

"But it does make you feel better. Believe me, I understand."

"Do you know a Mr Stenning?" Callie asked her.

"Of course I do, that man is an angel, we'd have even more problems with getting care for our elderly if he didn't help so many of them out."

"I think I may have to enlist his help with Violet Osbourne, she's desperate to get home."

"Sounds like a plan," Linda replied. As she turned to go, she said over her shoulder, "Oh and the very lovely young man who was here yesterday, Samuel Okojie, would like you to call him when you have a moment."

"Thank you, I'll do it straight away."

Callie picked up the phone and waited for Linda to leave before dialling. She felt a little anxious, despite Okojie's reassurances as he left that he believed her, and Kate's, side of the story.

"Dr Hughes, thank you for calling back," he said as soon as he picked up. "I just wanted you to know that the chair in charge of Dr Brown's hearing was inclined to reschedule it sooner rather than later. He agrees with me that this is just a delaying tactic. So, we will hopefully be getting back to you with a new date in the next week or so."

"Gosh, that was quick. I'll need a bit of notice to organise time off and cover again."

"Of course."

"What made the chair decide to reschedule so quickly?" she asked.

"To be honest, Dr Brown wasn't able to give any corroborating evidence for his version of events, unlike you."

"Well, that's hardly surprising. And what about Jessica Hemsworth? Is she still okay to put her side of the story?"

"Yes, I have spoken to her father as well, and he assures me that she will be."

There was something about his tone of voice that made Callie wonder if perhaps he realised that Jessica's father was more than a little anxious about the effect it might have on his daughter. Maybe Callie should call her and make sure she was still okay and knew she had support, because Callie was sure that she would need it.

* * *

"Did you tell Nigel about your trip to the care home?" Kate asked later. They had walked to The Stag after Kate had met Callie at the surgery, and the persistent drizzle meant they were very pleased to get there and see the fire blazing away. However, it was too warm to sit by the fire, so they had chosen a table near the window.

"Yes, he's busy checking into how Derek Childs bought the house. It may prove to be groundless gossip, but whatever, he was very relieved not to have had to go and talk to her himself."

"You do have to ask yourself if he is really a suitable candidate to be a policeman. I mean, he's such a sensitive soul."

"Of course he is. Nigel is a real asset to the police force," Callie told her indignantly. "And it's precisely because he isn't like the rest of them. He thinks in a completely different way, which means he gives them an added perspective."

"Hmm." Kate clearly wasn't convinced. "What about identifying the bones – are they any nearer?"

"It's going to be hard to definitively identify them. There don't seem to be any living relatives and none of their belongings remain anywhere that would give us a DNA match."

"They did manage to get DNA from the skeletons then?"

"Yes, but the chief superintendent doesn't want to pay the lab to do the more detailed analysis that might give us more."

"And no teeth for dental records?"

"Unfortunately not. It's not that uncommon a generation or two back, which isn't that helpful either."

"Bank account activity? Mobile phones? Anything to show they are alive?"

"Steve's trying to get search warrants for the bank, but he's meeting some resistance as he can't say for sure it's them." Callie sighed. "But two people disappearing off the face of the earth about the same time as two skeletons were buried in their garden – that's one hell of a coincidence if it isn't them."

"I'll say. So they definitely didn't go to the flash care place in Battle then?"

"There is no record of them going there, which makes me even more sure that they must have died before they could go."

Kate agreed and then glanced at her watch and started gathering her things together. "Sorry, but I'm going to have to love you and leave you. Let me just see you home."

"Hot date?" Callie asked as she quickly finished her sparkling mineral water; a choice that had made Kate wince when she ordered it.

"Oh yes, and I have you to thank for that," Kate replied.

"Really?" Callie queried.

"It's with Samuel Okojie."

"Oh, wow! He's a fast worker."

"I certainly hope so," Kate replied.

"Are lawyers allowed to go out with witnesses?"

"He says my corroboration isn't needed, so I'm not really a witness," Kate explained.

Callie thought it was uncomfortably close to doctors going out with patients, and perhaps it would have been better for them to wait until after the hearing, but she kept her thoughts to herself.

Despite Callie's protests that she could safely walk to Kate's cottage on her own, she allowed her friend to walk with her to the top of the road and watch until she was safely inside. With a quick wave, Callie went into the house and closed the door.

She couldn't help but feel a little bit envious of Kate's plans for the night. She was facing an evening on her own, well, on her own apart from Steve Miller camped out on the couch watching the football, with nothing but a microwave meal or yet another takeaway to look forward to – that and a phone call from Billy which would in the past have excited her, but now seemed almost a duty, a chore that needed to be done like laundry or tax returns.

They couldn't carry on a relationship in this way. It was time to make her mind up: either she needed to move to Belfast or he needed to come back to Hastings, and if neither was going to happen, then she had to accept that the relationship was over. Of that, she was sure. Now, she just needed to tell Billy, although it felt distinctly awkward, talking to him in the spare bedroom, with Miller watching television downstairs.

The phone call was a disaster. It was clear that Billy had no intention of coming back to England, for her or anyone else.

"I finally find a job that's fulfilling and everything I've wanted and you want me to drop it?" he had said, incredulous, when she suggested it. "What about you dropping your bloody job and coming over here?"

"I'd be leaving friends and family behind if I moved to Belfast," she had countered.

"I left my friends and family to come here too!"

"Yes, but you had a reason to leave them." Callie had known that was the wrong thing to say the moment the words were out of her mouth. The unspoken implication that Billy was not enough of a reason to move to Belfast, hung in the air and she scrabbled around for something more, a better reason for it not to be her who gave up everything.

"My parents are getting older, and I'm their only child," she said. "I need to be here." A long silence followed this, and she thought that he would call her out on this assertion. After all, her parents weren't that old, and they were perfectly capable. She also didn't see them that often. She was always happy to see her father, but avoided seeing her mother too much because it always left her feeling somehow inadequate. This was very different to Billy's family, who were much more close-knit.

"So that's it then?" was all he said. "You want to call it a day?"

The ease with which he said that panicked her slightly. She wanted him to be prepared to give up everything for her. She knew that wasn't reasonable, but she, in turn wasn't sure that she wanted to give up everything for him.

"No, I don't want to call it a day, but I don't even have a job over there," she said. "I'd go mad if I came over with nothing to do. Perhaps I'll contact that practice again, the one you said were looking to hire a new partner."

"No, they've probably filled the vacancy and I don't think they'd be a good fit for you anyway," he said quickly.

"Oh? What's happened to make you change your mind?"

"The senior partner's a bit of an ass, if I'm honest, and very scathing about the female partners, wants them to do all the women's problems and baby clinics. You'd hate him."

"I certainly would," she agreed, Billy knew how much she hated doing baby clinics.

"I'll ask around, though, see if any other jobs are going, ones that would suit you better, okay?" he had said but there was something in his voice that made her feel that he wouldn't put much effort into it. After all, he had tried before and she hadn't shown much interest.

Something had changed, she was sure, and not just because of her gaffe about needing a reason to move to Belfast. Perhaps he didn't really believe she was serious, and he didn't want to mess up his working relationship with the practice or any other contacts he had made. To be fair, she had said she was applying before and then pulled out. He couldn't keep telling them his girlfriend was interested in their post only for her not to apply for it.

And would she pull out again? Did she really want to make the move, even for Billy's sake?

She longed to call Kate and ask her opinion, but she couldn't disturb her hot date and anyway, she knew very well what her friend would say.

"If you have to ask yourself whether or not you want to be with Billy, the answer is you don't." Callie could almost hear her say it, and she knew her friend was, generally speaking, right, but it wasn't as simple as that. All those times he had been there for her, had cooked for her, had cared for her. The times they had laughed, the times they had cried; it wasn't easy to just dismiss them all. She owed it to him to give it a go.

* * *

She isn't making it easy for me. Taxis everywhere she goes and policemen hanging around everywhere, even sleeping over, protecting her. No, I'm going to have to think of something more elaborate, more inventive. But there is no doubt in my mind, I am not going to let it drop. I want to hurt her, I need to pay her back for what she has done. I need to frighten her and I will find a way to do it.

Chapter 16

"Good morning!" Linda said cheerily as she entered the office.

"Morning," Callie echoed, in a much less cheerful voice.

"Get out of bed the wrong side this morning, did we?"

"Yes," Callie replied and made her way to the small staff kitchen for a much-needed cup of coffee. There was nothing worse than someone who was cheerful in the morning, particularly when you were feeling out of sorts. She had slept fitfully, when she had slept at all. The nagging doubts about what she was thinking of doing had gone around and around in her head all night. She needed to try going to Belfast, for Billy's sake, but before that, she had to make sure she had a job to go to. She knew, all too well, that she couldn't ever be the sort of woman who sat at home waiting for her man. She would climb the walls with boredom. She was no housewife and Billy would die of malnutrition if the cooking was up to her. She needed a job if she was going to make a go of moving to be with Billy.

"There's nothing else for it," she told the coffee cup as she stirred it vigorously. "I need to go over there and see the situation for myself, maybe set up some interviews."

She already had Friday afternoon off, as that had been the original date for Dr Brown's hearing, and after a certain amount of wrangling with Gauri and Linda, she had managed to cancel her Friday morning clinic. As she wasn't on call over the weekend, she would be able to take a flight to Belfast on Thursday evening and wouldn't need to leave until late on the Sunday. Billy was working and on-call over the weekend, she knew, but they would be able to spend some time together, and she could busy herself getting to know Belfast better and job hunting. Having time on her own in the city might help her feel less like a tourist, she thought.

"Now all I've got to do is be patient," she told the cupboard, eliciting a strange look from one of the practice nurses who happened to be passing.

* * *

"Are you sure?" Kate asked her, when she told her friend her plans for the weekend.

"I have to try and make a go of it. I can't just let him go without a fight," Callie replied. "He deserves it, and I do too."

Kate seemed to realise that she didn't want to hear any negative views and kept quiet, although, from the look on her face, she had a few comments she wanted to make. Like: is he prepared to fight for it too? And isn't it too late in the day to save this relationship? Callie had asked herself exactly those questions too, but didn't have the answers.

"If you are going to rush off and leave me, I shall have to find someone else to share my weekend brunch, then." There was a ghost of a smile on Kate's lips.

"Like that's going to be a problem," Callie replied, glad to have got off the subject of Billy. "How was your date with the delightful Samuel?"

"Very delightful," Kate had a smug smile on her face that made Callie wish she hadn't asked.

"Did he tell you that they are sorting out a new date for Gerry's hearing?"

"No. Strangely, we didn't talk about work at all, but it's good to hear. The sooner that man is struck off the better, as far as I am concerned. Have you had any more trouble from him?"

"No, thank goodness, I'm hoping he understands that it is not a good idea."

"Yes, let's hope so."

But neither of them was quite convinced.

As soon as she had finished her morning list, Callie checked the NHS jobs website for any posts being advertised in Northern Ireland. There were several available, including one at the practice where Callie had applied previously, and not followed up when offered an interview. She wondered if Billy was right that the senior partner was some kind of misogynist.

She googled the practice and saw that there were several male partners, although none of them were named as senior, and also two female partners in the practice already. That meant that whichever of the men was the most senior, he couldn't have that much against women. Or perhaps, that women were employed to do the women's health and, horror of horrors, the baby clinics. All those screaming babies and anxious mothers, often with a badly-behaved toddler in tow as well. It was Callie's least favourite job.

She was happy with women's health sessions but endless obs and gynae work could and would end up boring her. What she liked most about being a GP was the variety, but even with that, she also liked being able to escape to the completely different role of police doctor.

She googled the police service in Northern Ireland and looked to see if they had any posts like that around Belfast. Whilst they certainly had forensic medical examiners, there were no posts being advertised. In general, like in England, a lot of the traditional police doctor role was being taken over by custody nurses and paramedics. The opportunities for being a police doctor were few and far between, but Callie hoped that she might find out more about how to get on the register to be one, once she was living and working there as a GP.

"Gauri?" Callie asked when they were both in the doctors' office alone at lunchtime.

"Yes?" Gauri responded cautiously.

"If I were to take a sabbatical, go and work in Northern Ireland, say for a year, would you keep my post here open for me to return?"

Gauri sighed.

"I can't make promises, I don't think, but given that we are one doctor short even with you here, I think you can be pretty sure that we would welcome you back with open arms if you decided to return. Particularly if you weren't always rushing off to act like a policeman, because I somehow doubt they would keep that post open for you."

She had a point, Callie conceded.

"And anyway," Gauri continued, "do you think it is wise to go over there with the idea that it's only short term? Is it not the case that you will be bound to fail if you are so unsure? Perhaps you shouldn't go at all."

"No, no," Callie hastily reassured her. "I wouldn't be planning on coming back, it's just comforting to think that I would have something to come back to if it didn't work out. Or if Billy got a job back here."

From the look Gauri gave her, it was clear she didn't believe Callie, and, to be fair, Callie wasn't sure she believed herself. As Gauri left to do her visits, Callie picked up the phone and called the surgery in Belfast where she had previously applied for a post. She wanted to speak to the female partner she had spoken to before, but she was unavailable. Callie did, however, manage to get through to one of the other partners, the other female one.

"Hello, my Name is Callie Hughes, I'm a GP in England and I just wanted to ask a few questions about the post for a doctor that you have advertised?"

"Oh yes, didn't you apply before? My name is Fiona Walsh, by the way, and I'm the senior partner here."

Callie was surprised to hear that; she was sure Billy had said that it was one of the men who was senior partner.

"We were so disappointed when you didn't follow through with your application," Fiona continued.

"Yes, I'm sorry about that. Circumstances stopped me moving forward." Circumstances like being unsure she wanted to move. Instead, Callie asked about how women and children's health issues were dealt with at the practice.

"None of us are specifically women's health partners and Dr Murphy does most of the baby clinics. He loves the little ones, wanted to be a paediatrician but found it too hard with the really sick ones. Why? Are you wanting to maybe specialise in women and children?"

"No, no," Callie hastily reassured her. "Just the opposite."

Fiona laughed. "Me too."

"Look," Callie confided, "I'm coming over to visit this weekend, and I was wondering if it would be okay to pop in on Friday maybe late morning? Have an informal chat?"

"Of course! I'll let them know. I'll be around, so do make sure you come and say hello."

Callie assured her she would and after a bit more discussion, all hugely reassuring to Callie, she ended her call and sent off the job application. It really wasn't hard because she had already sent it once, so didn't need to change anything, and she had liked Fiona Walsh so much, she knew she would be happy to work with her.

Billy would be delighted when she told him later that evening that she had made the first moves to come and join him.

Callie spent Thursday morning dealing with urgent phone calls from patients and then called for a taxi to take her to the police station. Nigel was adding information to a whiteboard when she came into the room and she went over to see what it was.

"Hello, Dr Hughes," he said, as he looked down at a piece of paper in his hand and went back to writing on what seemed to be a map of the street where the bones had been found.

"I'm just writing in the residents' details and dates they lived in each of the houses," he explained. "Makes it easier to know who was where and when this way."

Callie looked at the names and remembered she had intended to check and see who had been or still was registered with the surgery. Of course, she couldn't then use that as a reason to go and visit them, but she could at least see if any of them had a legitimate reason for her to call on them, like Violet Osborne. She had a moment of guilt that she hadn't followed up with her attempts to get her home either. There had been so much going on, she felt that she wasn't doing anything properly; not giving her work, her patients or her relationship the time and energy they deserved. And she hadn't been to see her parents in a while either.

Once Nigel had finished putting the names and dates on the board, Callie took a photo. She wouldn't have time to do anything today, but she could follow it up next week. First things first; she had to do an evening clinic and then she had a plane to catch so that she could make a start on sorting out the first of her problems: her relationship with Billy.

Chapter 17

Just as she finished up her paperwork after a busy evening surgery, Callie got a call from reception. Could she quickly see an extra? Callie checked her watch. She really didn't have time; she had brought her overnight case with her so that she could take a taxi straight to Gatwick and get the late plane to Belfast.

"I really can't," she told the receptionist. "I mean, is it urgent? Can anyone else see them?"

Callie heard the receptionist relay the request to someone and then there was some shouting.

"You tell her to come out here and talk to me. Now!"

The voice was masculine and with a sinking heart she recognised it as Mr Hemsworth as she hurried into the waiting room.

"What's happened? Is Jessica all right?" she asked anxiously.

"She's gone," he said, brandishing a note. "I'll kill him if he lays a hand on her!"

Callie took the note from him and quickly read it.

"She says there that she's going to see him and they are going to run away to together," he said. "It's totally ridiculous and I'm not going to let it happen, so you better give me his address right now."

"I don't think he's in Hastings anymore, Lewis," Callie told him. "After your threats he said he would stay away."

"I need be sure. I need to find her, for God's sake. If he's run off with her…" Mr Hemsworth couldn't even finish the sentence.

"Look, I'll go around to his address, the last one I know about, anyway and see if she's there–"

"I'm coming with you," he said and she could tell that he wasn't going to be dissuaded.

Callie turned to the receptionist. "If my taxi comes, can you ask him to wait?" Then she hurried out into the light drizzle that had just started.

Callie knew from Linda that after his marriage break-up, Gerry Brown had moved into a new flat above some shops between George Street and the sea front. She hurried along the pedestrian street, swerving and ducking to avoid umbrellas. When she got to the entrance, she found it was locked, of course. There were six flats in the building, all the bells were named bar one and none of the names were Brown. She rang the unnamed bell but there was no answer.

"Like I said," she told Mr Hemsworth. "I don't think he's living here at the moment."

He pushed past her and rang the bell again, and then every one of the bells, hoping someone would buzz him in. When there was no response at all, apart from a "bugger off" from a woman in one flat, he started banging on the door. People in the street were beginning to stop and stare, despite the rain.

"Mr Hemsworth, Lewis, she's not here—"

Just then Callie saw Jessica, looking tired, wet and miserable, walking towards them with a backpack slung over one shoulder.

"Jessica!" she called and ran towards the girl. She was quickly overtaken by the Jessica's father and he grabbed his daughter up in a hug.

"I've been so worried," he said.

"I'm sorry, Dad," Jessica said and burst into tears. They were oblivious to the rain, but Callie wasn't and suggested that they go into the nearest pub, to warm up and dry off. Callie checked her watch, the taxi to take her to the airport was due any minute, but she needed to know Jessica was all right before she left.

"What's all this about running away?" Callie asked her gently whilst Mr Hemsworth fetched some drinks, beer for himself and orange juice for Jessica.

"He said I had to promise not to go to the hearing thingy as he would need his licence to work. I knew Dad wouldn't let me just not turn up, so I thought I'd run away and be with him, but he wasn't there. He's gone away without me."

The misery on her face reminded Callie of the first time her heart had been broken.

"I know you don't want to hear all the stuff about how he's not worth it or you'll get over it in time, right now, but it really is true, Jessica."

The girl clearly didn't believe her but said nothing as Mr Hemsworth put the glasses on the table and sat down. He took Jessica's hand before speaking.

"He was just trying to get you to drop the complaint, pumpkin."

"He said he'd kill himself if he couldn't be a doctor and he couldn't be with me."

Mr Hemsworth patted her hand. "He's just saying that."

"He loves me," Jessica sobbed.

Callie and Lewis Hemsworth sat awkwardly as Jessica cried.

"How has he been communicating with you?" Callie asked.

Jessica looked at her dad and then back at Callie before fishing a cheap mobile phone out of her pocket.

"He gave it to me," she explained. "So we could message each other, but when I told him about running away and asked why he wasn't at home, he got cross and told me not to be so silly and to go home, and wait for him. I said I didn't want to, but he wouldn't listen. He said I would spoil everything and he wouldn't be able to keep his licence if they knew we were together."

"I know it's hard, Jessica," Callie said, "but he's just trying to stop you from telling your story and you have to do that."

"But if I do, he'll kill himself and then I'll kill myself!"

Jessica's distress was evident, and knowing her past history of self-harming, both Callie and her dad had to take her threat seriously.

"Look, I'll have a word with the lawyer and see if there's another way we can do this," Callie said, but she knew there wasn't. She glanced at her watch again. "I have to go now, but I'll talk to you both before the hearing, okay?" She looked at them and got a nod from Mr Hemsworth.

"Thanks, Dr Hughes," he said.

"And remember, Jessica, your dad loves you, no matter what and he knows a lot about people, so maybe this time, he's right."

As she went to leave the pub, Mr Hemsworth came to the door, keeping his eyes on his daughter all the time.

"I don't know that I can make her do it," he told Callie. "I can't risk it even if it means he does it again, to someone else's daughter."

"I know," she said. "I understand. I really do."

She left them in the pub and ran back to the surgery. The taxi was waiting outside, and she waved at him.

"Won't be a moment," she said before running in and picking up her weekend bag, hoping that she still had enough time to catch her flight.

As the driver set off, Callie took out her phone and called Kate.

"Are you at the airport?" Kate asked.

"On my way, and running a bit late," she explained.

"God, you're cutting it a bit fine."

"I know. I got held up," Callie replied and glanced at the driver in front of her. "Jessica ran away to be with Gerry and I had to find her before I left."

"Jessica ran away with him?"

"Tried to, but he wasn't there, thank goodness, although when she rang him, he wasn't best pleased. Anyway, I found her and returned her to her dad's care, but I'm not sure if he's going to be able to persuade her to turn up at the hearing. She threatened to hurt herself and it's shaken him," Callie replied and was slightly taken aback to hear whispering at the other end.

"Um, Callie?" a voice that was definitely not Kate's asked. "It's Samuel Okojie here."

Callie had guessed as much and couldn't help but smile. She was glad Kate had taken the chance to see Samuel while Callie wasn't there, and, more importantly, there wasn't a policeman asleep on her sofa. She hadn't known who was more relieved when she said she was going to Belfast, Kate or Steve Miller.

"So, you think she won't come to the hearing?" Samuel asked.

"Well, I think it's unlikely."

"And there has been contact between the two of them?" he asked.

"He gave her a mobile phone that her dad didn't know about and they've been messaging."

A glance at the driver told her that he was listening to every word and was intrigued by the call. "Look, I can't really talk about it now. I was going to ask you to contact Samuel, but clearly that's not necessary now."

"No," Samuel replied. "Look, leave it with me, I'll talk to the board chair and see what he has to say."

"Thanks, Samuel," she replied, knowing full well that without a complainant there wasn't much they could do.

"And have a great weekend away," Kate added.

"Thanks," Callie said and ended the call, but as the taxi turned onto the A27 the traffic ground to a halt and there was nothing but the glaring red of brake lights stretching out in front of them.

"Bit of a jam," the driver said apologetically and Callie sighed. There was no way she was going to catch the plane she was booked on.

Chapter 18

Callie arrived in Belfast early the next morning, having spent the night in a hastily booked, cheap hotel close to Gatwick. Billy was working so he couldn't meet her at the airport. He had taken the news that she'd missed her flight the night before calmly, as if he had half-expected it, which, in turn, had left her wondering if she let people down so often it had become normal. She didn't think so, but...

She was also disappointed not to be able to spend a romantic night catching up with him, and telling him of her plans to join him in Belfast before she set about job hunting. He had even suggested that perhaps it wasn't a good time to be coming because he was busy at work and there were clearly a lot of things going on in Hastings. But she had brushed his suggestion aside. She needed to see him, she said, but didn't tell him the reason. She wanted to see him in person for that.

She wanted a romantic evening in to talk about the future, so she planned to do a bit of shopping and buy something that simply needed reheating and arranging on a plate, given her culinary skills, and a bottle of wine. Perhaps she should buy some candles as well, she mused as she dumped her bag in the hallway of Billy's flat.

Despite having lived there for more than six months, the flat still had the air of being unlived-in, apart from the kitchen, which had always been Billy's domain. His idea of winding down after a hard day dissecting dead bodies was to cut up some meat and vegetables and turn them into something delicious. Callie tried hard, but somehow her efforts were never as good.

Having checked the kitchen cupboards and the fridge and seen that there were lots of ingredients but nothing ready-made, she sent Billy a quick text to let him know she had arrived safely and told him she was going out for a walk and a spot of sightseeing.

Callie had made a note of the address of the practice she had applied to join and worked out a route that would be a pleasant half-hour walk, provided the rain held off.

She could stop at the shops on the way back and buy something suitable for the meal when she would tell him about her application to the practice and that she had been there. Maybe then he would believe that she really meant to move in with him this time. Maybe then he would be happy.

On her walk out of the centre of Belfast and towards the surgery, Callie was disturbed to see signs that the city was still not fully at peace: high walls covered with razor wire, fences with nets above to stop stones or other missiles being thrown over and flags everywhere declaring that particular area's allegiances. She had seen some of this when she had visited Billy before, particularly when they had visited Derry and walked the old town walls, but she found it depressing all the same. Did she really want to work in such a divided community? She had timed her walk so that she would arrive at the end of morning clinics, when, hopefully, someone would be free to talk to her and perhaps show her around the premises.

She was relieved to find that it was not in one of those worryingly fortified areas; instead it was situated on the corner of a nice-looking residential street. It was a large Victorian building, which had a more modern extension on the side. It looked well-cared for and newly painted, and there were no fences or missile shields around the building, she was relieved to see.

She stopped and held the door open for a woman who was trying to leave the building with a double-wide pushchair and another small child hanging on to the side. With Callie flattened against the wall, clutching the door, the woman did eventually manage to get out and muttered a quick thanks before setting off along the road, a determined look on her face. Callie could only imagine the organisation needed to handle three small children like that.

Callie went into the waiting area and approached the young woman behind the screened reception desk, pleased to see a smile of welcome as she approached.

"Hello," she said, "is Dr Walsh free?"

"She's finished her morning clinic but I could make you an appointment for tonight if it's urgent? Or next week if not?"

"I'm not a patient," Callie explained. "I spoke to her about a possible job vacancy here and said I might be coming over to Belfast. She said to pop in and look around the surgery if I did. I'm Dr Hughes, Callie Hughes? I know I should have called first, but I just wanted to maybe have a chat if she has a moment?"

The receptionist quickly relayed this message to the main office and Callie found herself being taken through to the back of the building where the main offices were.

"Dr Hughes, is it?" A comfortably built, middle-aged woman asked as she came forward, holding out her hand. "I'm Maggie, the practice manager. Were we expecting you?"

"No, not really," Callie assured her as they shook hands. "It's just that I'm here in the city seeing my boyfriend and I thought I'd take a walk and come and see what the practice was like. I hope you don't mind?"

"Of course not, that's very sensible of you. You're moving over from England, are you?" Maggie was leading Callie through the busy office towards the back door which seemed to lead to the kitchen and a smaller office. Callie could feel every eye on her as she passed the office staff.

"That's right," Callie said.

"Dr Walsh? There's a Dr Hughes here to see you," the practice manager announced as she opened the office door.

A woman stood up and walked towards her. Callie recognised her as Dr Walsh from the photos on the website. She must have been in her late fifties and had a no-nonsense look about her, with her salt-and-pepper hair, tweed skirt, and half-moon glasses on a chain round her neck.

"Dr Hughes, welcome. Glad you were able to get over here to come and see us. Let me introduce you to some of my colleagues and then, perhaps" – she looked at Maggie the practice manager – "someone could show you around the practice?"

Maggie nodded. "Of course, I'll just see who's free." Maggie left the room and Fiona started to introduce Callie to everyone else.

"Dr Hughes has sent in an application to join as a new partner, and wanted to pop in for a chat before we get to anything so formal as an interview. This is Dr O'Leary." She pointed at a young man in his thirties who stood and held his hand out with a smile of welcome.

"Patrick," he said as they shook. "Pat, if you like, but never Paddy."

Callie made a mental note as she shook hands with the next doctor she was introduced to, and then finally the only other female doctor.

"And this is Dr Alison McCauley."

Alison McCauley also stood and briefly shook hands. She was younger than Fiona, well-dressed and with blond hair cut in a neat and expensive-looking style. She managed a brief, nervous smile in response to the introduction.

"Sorry," she said as she hastily bundled her paperwork together and picked up her bag. "I didn't know we were expecting visitors and I have to go."

"Of course, I quite understand," Callie told her. "I know what it's like. I should have made an appointment, but I didn't want it to be anything too formal."

Alison nodded agreement and left the room, not exactly hostile, but not friendly either.

"Sorry, I know I must be in the way," Callie apologised.

"It's not a problem at all," Fiona said and looked at Maggie who had just returned.

"I'll show you around the place myself, if you like?" Maggie offered.

"That would be very good of you. I won't take up too much of your time, I promise."

With a small wave at the remaining doctors who were already turning back to their work, Callie followed Maggie out of the office. The tour didn't take long. The building reminded Callie of her old surgery in Hastings, where she had worked before they moved to the new premises. Trying to coax old buildings into premises fit for the 21st century was always a nightmare in that the layout was not ideal, with rooms leading off rooms and with small messy waiting areas fitted in wherever they could be. But despite all the inadequacies, it seemed a good practice and Callie got a sense that everyone was happy working there. She might still have niggling doubts after her time spent exploring the city and the obvious tensions around, but the practice itself had not thrown up any hurdles great enough to make her decide not to come over and work there. It would be a challenge, of course, but not an insurmountable one. And if it didn't work out, she could always go back to Hastings.

* * *

"So, let me get this right," Kate said over the telephone later as Callie busied herself chopping vegetables for her romantic dinner with Billy. The wine, the most important part as far as she was concerned, was in the fridge chilling. "You are planning on renting out your flat, moving in with Billy, working at a practice over there while still keeping your job open at the surgery, so that, in fact, everything is still in place in case it doesn't work out and you want to come back?"

"Yes," Callie replied. "And I know what you are going to say next too."

"Oh yes? What's that?"

"That I am making plans as if I expect to fail."

"Well, yes, that's exactly what I was going to say. And," she added, "if you expect your plans to fail, they will."

116

Just like Gauri had told her.

"But I do need to give it a shot, Kate, to make Billy see that I have tried to save our relationship, that I haven't just given up on him at the first hurdle. I would feel such a failure if I didn't at least try, if that makes sense?"

"Yes, I do see, and it does," she said with an audible sigh. "But it's quite a big gesture, just to try and stop yourself from feeling guilty, and is it fair on Billy if you haven't really got your heart in it?"

* * *

Callie was on the phone to Jayne Hales when Billy finally came home, and as he was later than she had expected, she had already started on the wine. She waved at him and tilted her head for him to kiss on the cheek before returning to her conversation.

"Is there any news on trying to trace the Childses?"

"Absolutely zilch," Jayne replied. "It's looking more and more likely that it is them, though. The pathologist has confirmed that they are the right age and size to fit with the skeletons, but we may never be a hundred percent sure it is them. Now the question is, how did they die and who buried them?"

"Exactly. Were they still getting pensions?"

"Apparently," Jayne replied. "You'd have thought someone would have checked they were still alive, but clearly not. Nigel managed to get the warrant to examine the Childses' finances and found that the pensions go into an account in Derek's name, where the money from the sale of the house was also deposited. The balance has steadily declined since then. In fact, there's only a few thousand left in there, or rather…" There was a short pause as she obviously checked her facts. "The account has £5,163.46 in it."

Callie was a bit distracted as Billy had wandered into the kitchen. She hoped she hadn't left too much of a mess in there.

"When was the most recent withdrawal?"

"Earlier this year. About two months ago."

There were a few moments of silence as Callie digested this fact, then there was the sound of the oven door opening and Billy taking the casserole out.

"But if the bones are them, they must have been dead well before that. Like years before."

"I know," Jayne said. "It can't have been them taking the money out."

"Do we have any idea who is?"

"That would be good, wouldn't it? But no, we don't because the money was taken out, in dribs and drabs, from cash machines. No big transfers into other accounts or anything handy like that. I've got Nigel mapping exactly where the cash machines were located as we speak."

There was a clatter from the kitchen and a disconcerting smell of burnt food wafted into the room.

"Would there be CCTV pictures if it was only a month or two back?" Callie asked.

"We're looking into it, but..." Jayne clearly wasn't hopeful and had nothing more of interest to tell her.

"I know, these things take time."

"Nigel got the address on register at both the bank and the DWP, and it's still the old house, which we know is out of date. It seems they had requested only electronic notifications and statements and Nigel is busy trying to find out more about the email address they used."

Callie's mind was still on her conversation with Jayne as she ended the call and went into the kitchen, where Billy was now busy putting the casserole dish into the sink and running water into it. A cloud of smoke and steam rose up from the sink with a hiss.

"Sorry," Callie said and reached out for him but the smoke alarm went off, and she covered her ears instead.

"Wow! That's loud!" she said as Billy reached up to silence it. As soon as the beeping stopped, Billy opened the windows to let the smoke out.

"Gosh, I'm so sorry. Hope we haven't upset the neighbours." She laughed. When Billy turned back to her she expected to see him laughing too and teasing her about what a hopeless cook she was, like he often did, but instead his expression was angry.

"This is the last thing I need!" he shouted and threw the tea towel at her and stormed out of the room.

"I'm sorry," she said quietly, stunned by his over-the-top reaction. "I just got distracted. It's only a casserole dish. I'll get another."

"It's not the dish, for God's sake! Forget about the bloody dish. I am just tired of you always being busy with something else," he said. "Never me," he added quietly.

His shoulders sagged and he rubbed a spot between his eyes. Callie said nothing; this anger from him was so out of character, so out of the blue, that she wasn't sure what she should say, or do.

"I'm sorry, it's just that I'm tired and hungry," he explained, shoulders sagging, no longer angry, but, worse than that, disappointed in her. "The last thing I needed was another drama."

"We can call for a takeaway…"

"No, I need–" He struggled to find the right words. "I don't need this." He waved in her direction and the kitchen.

"I wanted to cook you a romantic meal, to make up for not seeing you for so long."

"It has been long," he said, "too long. And you just waltz back in here, ruining my kitchen, expecting everything to be as it was. Well, things aren't the same and I can't do this anymore."

She couldn't understand where all this was coming from, what he was really saying.

"I'm sorry, I'll clean the kitchen tomorrow."

"It's not that, I mean, for God's sake, when were you going to tell me about applying for the job, when I tried to warn you against doing that?"

"I was going to tell you tonight. I wanted to surprise you. I thought you'd be happy."

"Well, that's one more thing you've got wrong, isn't it? I'm sorry, I really can't do this now." He walked to the door, picking up his bag and his coat on the way.

"Where are you going?"

"I'll stay the night somewhere else. We'll talk in the morning." He opened the front door.

"Please don't go, Billy. Let's talk about it now, I need to know what's wrong. What I've done to upset you."

"No," he said firmly. "Tomorrow." And he left.

At a loss to know what she should do once he had gone, and still shocked by his over-the-top reaction to what was to her mind a rather minor incident, Callie decided to tackle the kitchen first. Cleaning was always her go-to activity when she was troubled and needed to think things through. Cleaning or walking. But it was late, very dark outside with a steady rain and she didn't know the area, didn't know where was safe to walk at night, so cleaning it was.

The state of the kitchen wasn't as bad as she expected. The casserole was beyond help, so she threw that out, and once the last of the smoke had cleared, she cleaned the oven and wiped all the surfaces down. With a shiver, she closed the window and wondered where Billy had gone. A hotel perhaps? But she didn't think so. Some things were beginning fall into place. His recent lack of interest. His sudden loss of temper.

Deciding that wine, whilst tempting, would be a bad idea – she needed a clear head – Callie made herself a mug of tea and sat on the sofa in the living room, going over and over recent events and conversations with Billy.

How had he known about her visit to the surgery that lunchtime? Of course, any one of the doctors could have spoken to him, if they knew him and about his relationship with her, but none of them had mentioned Billy, or shown that they knew him, and she had said nothing about the fact that she was in a relationship with the pathologist.

She thought more about her visit to the practice, the friendliness of all the staff, well, almost all of the staff. How Dr Alison McCauley – the young, stylish, good-looking Dr Alison McCauley – had left so abruptly when she was introduced. Even her colleagues had been surprised by her departure, she felt. So why had she walked out? Callie was beginning to have her suspicions, but she didn't want to believe them. Was she just being paranoid? She certainly hoped so, but her gut didn't agree.

She went around the flat, looking at things methodically, searching for proof, one way or another. The bed had been made up with fresh sheets, so there was nothing to see there. Billy had a very good cleaner so there was no lingering smell of perfume anywhere in the flat, no smells at all apart from bleach and burnt dinner. There were no earrings or make-up lying around, no bra hidden behind a sofa cushion, no obvious sign of another woman. Then she found it in the vanity bin in the bathroom: a tampon wrapper from a make she didn't use. In fact, two wrappers.

Of course, Billy could have had friends or colleagues around for dinner or a drink and one of them could have left a wrapper in the bin, but two? They would have had to be there some time, like overnight, she thought.

She went through the evidence like a list: the tampon wrappers, Billy's change in attitude, his knowledge of her visit to the practice and, finally, how he had blown up at such a minor event. It was, to Callie, enough proof that something was going on. She could, and probably should, stay and have it out with him in the morning, but somehow, she didn't think she could face it.

Callie changed her return flight to the first one available, collected her bag, and added the very few personal bits and pieces she had left in the flat when she had visited previously, nothing very much, as she had been there only a few times since he had moved in. Then she called for a taxi to take her to the airport.

* * *

I am watching her flat from my usual hiding place. The lights came on at eight o'clock, but I know that is just because they are on a timer, set to make people think she was at home, even if she isn't. And she clearly isn't, I can feel it. She isn't here. I am all set up for her and she isn't here. I am so frustrated that I throw the acid I have brought with me over her stupid, stupid car. At least she will know I am still around, that I am still out to get her. Next time I come with a bottle of acid, I will pour it on her, I promise myself, and I leave her a note to make sure she gets the message. She will be next.

Chapter 19

"Well, this is an unexpected surprise," Kate said as she answered the door, dressed in a scarlet silk bathrobe decorated with gold dragons. Callie could hear movement upstairs; Kate clearly wasn't alone.

"I'm sorry, I should have called, I'll come back later." Callie turned and would have left but Kate, realising that all was not well, stopped her.

"Don't be silly." She enveloped her friend in a hug. "I'm guessing you didn't have the romantic reunion with Billy you were hoping for." She pulled Callie into the house and closed the door. "Now, tell me what's wrong."

"He's having an affair, I know he is!" Callie sobbed. She was never normally overemotional, but her unhappiness was so great that this, the first sympathy she had been given, was too much for her and she broke down.

"Shhh." Kate pulled her into another hug and stroked her hair, letting her sob.

Once she had cried herself out, Kate sat her down.

"I'll make some coffee," she said and then went into the kitchen. There was a bit of creaking on the stairs and Samuel Okojie appeared, fully dressed, and with a slightly embarrassed smile.

"I will leave you two ladies," he said.

"Oh no, please don't go on my account. I'll go." Callie grabbed her bag and was heading to the door when Kate stopped her.

"No, you don't. You are not leaving my house in that sort of a state," Kate told her firmly, grabbing the bag and leading her back to the sofa. "You look a right mess."

Callie couldn't help but smile, even though she knew it was probably true.

"I have to go back to London, anyway," Samuel explained to her. "I'll call later," he said to Kate with a grin. She blew a kiss at him and he left.

"I'm so sorry to have spoiled your Saturday morning lie-in," Callie said and blew her nose.

"Like he said, he has to go, and anyway, that's what friends are for, isn't it? Now, tell me all about it. What makes you think Billy is having an affair?"

Callie told her and Kate didn't try to tell her she was mistaken.

"You need to talk to him," was all she said. "Has he called you?"

Callie held up her phone.

"Flat battery," she explained. "What with everything going on, I didn't get around to charging it."

Kate fetched a charging cable and plugged the phone in. After a moment or two, a number of messages and missed calls, on both voicemail and WhatsApp, appeared on the display.

"Good job you don't have sound notifications," Kate said, "your phone would be dinging like mad."

Callie managed a small smile at this.

"I'll go upstairs and get dressed while you listen to them, then we can decide whether to stay in or go out so you don't sit there snivelling. Whatever you need to do, let me know. I can book a table or get a gallon of wine in and you can drink and weep all night," Kate said, leaving her to listen to the messages on her own.

She picked up her phone and braced herself. She would start with the text messages. She didn't think she could cope with hearing his voice right now. She would need to at some point, she knew that, but she didn't feel strong enough just yet. She opened the most recent message from him. It said that he was sorry, and that he hadn't wanted to end it this way. That was really everything she needed to know, without having to hear or read his other, longer messages. She could sort out the details later, hear his excuses for having fallen for somebody else, about being lonely, that she was never there for him. It was all too raw at the moment. She didn't need him to put the blame on her because a little bit of her felt that he would be right. She had chosen to stay in Hastings, but she wasn't the one who had been unfaithful. Come Monday she would have to withdraw her application, again, and tell Gauri that she was staying. Hopefully, she would be pleased.

Leaving the messages, she checked her emails. Amongst the post waiting for her was a new date for the hearing with Gerry Brown, sent before the news that Jessica might withdraw her complaint and that he had been in touch with her despite being told that he should not. She wondered if the hearing would still go ahead. She supposed that would depend on what Samuel told the board and what he advised them to do if Jessica didn't turn up. She suspected the advice would be to drop the hearing and reinstate Gerry. It all seemed such a massive waste of everybody's time and he would be free to carry on destroying people's lives. In fact, he would probably feel vindicated.

Callie knew she needed to do something to take her mind off her problems and past experience had told her that Kate did not appreciate it when Callie cleaned her house.

"Do you fancy a walk?" she asked her friend when she reappeared downstairs. Kate sighed, walking was not a favourite pastime but she knew that Callie needed to clear her head.

"I'll just put on my walking shoes," she said and removed her leopard-print ankle boots with heels that would hinder safe walking. Callie wouldn't even attempt to walk around town in heels that high. She looked out of the window and noted the clouds scudding across the sky.

"Would you mind if we made a quick stop at my flat to pick up a fleece and a waterproof jacket?" she asked.

Kate paused as she pulled on her walking boots.

"If it rains, I will run to the nearest pub for shelter. I am a fair-weather walker, as you know all too well."

"I don't think it's going to rain," Callie reassured her. "But I do like to be prepared in case. We can go as soon as my phone has charged up."

* * *

The plan was to walk across the cliffs to Fairlight, keeping as close to the sea as they could and only dipping inland when the paths were closed because of landslides, which seemed to happen fairly regularly.

Having collected a fleece and waterproof jacket, and then added a bottle of water and some energy bars to a backpack from Callie's flat, they walked past her car towards the country park. Kate stopped and turned.

"What's that?" she said and went towards the car.

The first thing to catch Callie's eye was a piece of paper tucked under the windscreen wiper, but as Kate reached for it she saw that there was a patch of blistered and discoloured paint on the bonnet.

"Stop!" Callie shouted quickly and Kate pulled back her hand. She looked at the area that Callie was pointing to and realised its significance.

Someone had thrown paint-stripper or some kind of acid over the car and, had she leaned across to get the note, Kate might have touched it. Callie reached for her phone, all thoughts of a relaxing walk in the countryside gone.

* * *

It was a weekend and the only member of CID on duty and available was Nigel. At least he was happy to help; delighted, in fact, as being the resident IT guru meant that he rarely got a chance to get out of the office.

"I thought you were away this weekend, Dr Hughes?" he said when he arrived and looked at the damaged car.

"Yes, well, I had to come home early."

Nigel shuffled his feet.

"I'll have to tell DI Miller you're back," he said.

"That's fine," she reassured him. "I would have told him later anyway," she lied, knowing that he would be back on the sofa making sure she was safe tonight. Although she hated him having to do this, she had to admit it was reassuring.

"Now you're here, Nigel," Kate said. "I'll leave Callie in your safe hands and go back and get on with a few bits I need to do. Make sure you bring her back to my house, okay?"

"Of course."

They both knew there was no way Nigel would let Callie out of his sight, just in case anything happened to her. Miller would never forgive him if he did.

Once Kate had gone, Callie turned back to her car.

"The uniform sergeant who was here earlier said he'd try and arrange for forensics to come out but it probably wouldn't be until tomorrow," she told Nigel.

Nigel looked up to the sky.

126

"It might rain before then," he said.

"Exactly," Callie responded and looked pointedly at the note, still on her windscreen. "I don't want anything written on it to be indecipherable."

"I'll get an evidence bag," Nigel said, going back to the little car he had arrived in. It was a sort of dark mustardy yellow and Callie could only assume it had been cheap, because she couldn't think of any other reason someone would buy a car that colour. Unless they were colour blind.

Callie pulled on the gloves that Nigel returned with and gingerly leant over the car to reach the note and pull it out from under the windscreen wiper blade.

Opening it out, with Nigel looking over her shoulder, she read what the note said in bold capitals: "*YOU ARE NEXT.*"

"Hmm," was Nigel's only comment as she refolded the note with a shiver and dropped it into the evidence bag he was holding open.

"No news on finding Zac, I take it?" she asked him.

"Not as far as I know," he replied and looked towards her front door. "I don't suppose your doorbell video covers this area."

"No, I'm afraid not. That's the downside of having a front door on the side of the house, all it gets is the person standing in front of it and some bushes behind them. I thought about putting a CCTV camera in my front window to cover this area but somehow never got around to it, but I will. First thing tomorrow." She sighed. "My insurance premium is rising by the minute, not to mention the taxi bill."

"A camera would seem a sensible idea," he said.

"Maybe with one I could come home, stop disrupting my friends' lives."

"I'm not sure the DI would like that." Nigel seemed anxious at the idea. He certainly wouldn't want to be the one to tell his boss she had moved back home. "Could you go and stay with your parents?" he suggested helpfully, or so he clearly thought.

Too tired to explain just why that wasn't a good idea, Callie stopped and gave it some further thought. If she stayed at Kate's, she was definitely getting in the way of her friend's love life, and Steve Miller had enough on his plate without having to try and sleep on a sofa. There was a limit to how long she could put them both out like this. Besides, she suddenly had a longing for the safety of her childhood home and the comfort of parental love. Goodness only knew why, she had never actually found them in the least bit comforting when she was growing up.

"You're right. If you can just wait there while I get a few bits together and then get my bags from Kate's, you can drop me at the hire car place and I'll go to my parents' house," she told Nigel, decisively. "I can't see him following me all the way out there." At least she hoped not; she really couldn't take any more of this.

* * *

"Of course, you are always welcome, darling, you know that. I'm just saying that a bit of notice would not have gone amiss."

True to form, Callie hadn't been in the house ten minutes and there was already tension. Maybe it hadn't been such a good idea to go back there, particularly as she had had to hire a car to do so.

"I know, I'm sorry. I'm not staying tonight, I just wanted to drop my things off."

Diana looked at the case Callie had brought into the house.

"This is unexpected," she said.

"Yes, it's a long story, but is it okay if I stay for while? Not tonight, I'm having dinner with Kate in town and I'll probably stay at hers, but from tomorrow?"

"Of course, darling." Diana visibly held herself back from the comment about using the house like a hotel that

Callie had been expecting. "Will you be here for lunch tomorrow? I'm doing a roast, all the trimmings, so—"

"That would be lovely, Mummy."

"And will Billy be visiting at all?" Diana asked hopefully. She had very quickly got over her concerns about different cultures once she had met him and discovered he was a doctor; in fact she had fast become one of Billy's greatest fans.

"Er, no," Callie answered quickly, not yet feeling able to talk freely about it with her mother. "I'll just go and take my suitcase upstairs, out of your way and then I'll pop out and see Daddy."

"I'll make coffee and then you can take some out to him, save me one job, at least." Diana knew better than to push her daughter, but the shrewd look she was giving her meant that Callie was going to have to come clean soon and face the inevitable lecture on not getting any younger and needing to settle down.

She made her way carefully down the lane to her father's workshop, carrying the tray of coffee and biscuits her mother had handed her when she came back downstairs.

Charles Hughes had been bored and depressed when he first retired from being an orthopaedic surgeon, but then he had developed a love for motorcycles. Not riding them so much as taking old wrecks – 'classics' as he called them – and doing them up. He always seemed to have at least one bike in pieces when she visited, sometimes several.

Callie was pleased that he had been able to rent a suitable property nearby. He'd been travelling to a village several miles away before, not far but too far to just pop in from home. Callie thought that part of the charm of the place was that Diana couldn't just pop in and disturb him, but equally, as he was getting older, her father liked being closer to home and a regular supply of coffee. She put the tray on the step and opened the door.

"Hi, Dad," she called, "I've brought coffee."

"Ah, the prodigal returns," Charles Hughes said with a big welcoming smile, looking up from whatever it was he was working on, laid out on the workbench. "Has your mother killed the fatted calf?"

"Not quite, but I think she's planning to," Callie replied.

"And to what do we owe this unexpected visit?" he asked once she had poured him a cup of black coffee from the cafetière and handed it to him.

"I seem to have upset someone," she replied.

"Again?" he asked and listened as she explained all about her recent problems.

"I went to stay with Billy but it seems that, well, I think we are splitting up." She had finally listened to Billy's answerphone messages once she had decided to go to her parents and was all packed ready to go. Just in case she had got it wrong, she told herself. But she hadn't. He admitted that he had started seeing Alison McCauley, just as someone to go out for a drink with at first, but then as something more. He was sorry. He hadn't meant for it to happen, but it had.

"Ah, I did wonder," her father said when she told him. "Is that a *think* you are splitting up?" he asked gently, "or a *know* you are splitting up?"

"Know. He has been seeing someone else."

"Ah." He paused for a moment, thinking carefully about what his response should be, something that her mother rarely did. She would have jumped straight in with a comment about it hardly being surprising and probably all Callie's fault. "Well, I think it's a very good thing that you've come home for a bit of TLC." Although they both knew she probably wouldn't be getting much in the way of tender loving care, as her mother definitely believed in tough love. She would probably have set Callie up with a couple of blind dates with local eligible bachelors before the week was out.

* * *

Later, when she had met up with Kate in the wine bar, they laughed at the memories of the totally awful men Callie's mother had tried to set her up with in the past.

"What was the name of the bloke with a burping fetish?" Kate asked.

"Adrian," Callie replied. "But he came from such a good family, darling," she said, imitating her mother's voice. "That aside, he was just awful."

"You can always come back and stay with me," Kate told her. "You know you will never stick it out in the same house as your mother. I give it two days max."

"You know me too well, but what about Samuel? I don't want to be a gooseberry."

"He's busy at work all week, so I will only ever see him at weekends, anyway." She sipped her glass of red wine. "You could just go and stay with your parents when he comes."

"And then there is you having to come and collect and take me to work every day as well and Steve sleeping on your sofa. It's too much, Kate. Not to mention that I could be putting you in danger."

Reluctant as she was to accept this, Kate had to concede that Callie was making sense.

"I take it you will be staying at mine tonight, though." Kate nodded towards the large glass of white wine that Callie had ordered for herself.

"If that's okay, yes."

"Of course, it is."

"Thank you."

"Did you listen to Billy's messages?"

"Yes, and yes, I was right, he is seeing someone else. A GP over there, and yes, I'm sad and angry but also a little relieved. My decision has been made for me. I'm staying put."

"Cheers to that," Kate said and they clinked glasses.

"There is one proviso to me coming back to yours tonight, though," she told her friend.

"Oh yes?" Kate raised an eyebrow.

"I'd rather not talk about Billy."

"Of course. I have a voodoo doll for you to stick pins in instead."

"You have a voodoo doll?" Callie couldn't quite believe what she was hearing.

"Of course, I find it helpful when I'm competing with another woman for the same man."

"It's a female doll? I'm not sure I want to hurt the other woman. After all, it's not her I'm angry with, it's him."

"It can change, I have accessories."

"You have a voodoo doll with accessories?" Callie didn't know why she was surprised; it was somehow entirely in character.

"It's actually a kids' toy, with a number of different outfits and wigs so that I can picture it as whoever I want it to be." She had a sort of dreamy look as she thought about it. "Lots of outfits and an awful lot of pinholes."

Callie shook her head. It made a weird kind of sense.

They didn't have a late night, it had been an eventful day and Callie was almost asleep by the time their food arrived, so Kate took her home for a cup of cocoa and early bed.

Next morning, Callie got up early and made herself a peaceful cup of tea as Kate slept on. There was a ring at the door and Callie cautiously opened it to see Steve Miller standing there with a face like thunder.

"You should have called me," he said as he came inside. "Nigel said you'd gone to your parents' place."

"I have; for a short while, anyway. I just stayed last night with Kate because we were out in town and I'd had a drink."

"Oh." The wind seemed to have been taken out of his sails. "I'm not sure being out on the town's a good idea. Is Kate here? I'm surprised she let you answer the door on your own."

"She sleeps like a log, I doubt a hurricane would wake her."

"All the more reason for you to go home to your parents. I can't imagine anyone getting in there."

"No. Absolutely nothing gets passed my mother," she said.

"I thought you were going out to Belfast, anyway. What happened?"

"Long story." And one she really didn't want to go into right now, and definitely not with him. "Tea?" she asked, changing the subject and knowing full well that, unlike her, he preferred coffee in the mornings.

By the time she had made tea for herself and a pot of coffee for him, Kate had surfaced in her dragon-covered robe and was sitting next to Miller.

"Morning," Callie said as she busied herself handing out cups and pouring coffee.

"Life saver," Kate said as she cradled the cup in her hands and took a sip. She really did look as though she needed it.

Callie turned to Miller.

"Do you have any idea where Zac is? Or why he seems able to walk round town and harass me so freely?"

Miller grimaced. Callie wasn't sure if the coffee was distasteful or her question.

"Everyone has his picture, but he hasn't been seen anywhere in the Old Town. We've been tapping our intel sources, but they all seem to suggest he's busy taking back his old territory, not wandering around trying to get at you."

"But there's plenty of evidence to show that's exactly what he is doing. My car will probably never be the same again, always supposing I can afford to insure it after this." She put her hand on his to emphasise her point. "I need you to find him, Steve. I need you to put a stop to this, because I can't take this disruption to my life much longer."

Chapter 20

Callie had spent most of Sunday morning at the surgery. She was working her way through the photo she had taken of Nigel's chart that showed who had lived where in the street where the bones had been found, and, more importantly, when they had lived there. Callie had noted down who had been living in the row of sixteen houses during the time period when the bones must have been buried. Then, she checked the list of names against the surgery records. Unsurprisingly, they had all been registered with her practice. Several had died, and many had moved away, their records being sent to their new doctors and of the names on her list, only Violet Osborne was still a resident of the street. However, Terence Waldron, who now lived three doors down from the burial site, had the same surname as the person who had lived there twenty years earlier. A quick check suggested that he had taken over the council tenancy from his parents when they died.

He would have been a young man when the Childses disappeared, but she thought that he might still be worth interviewing. Checking his medical record, she found several things that she could use as an excuse. He was an overweight, type two diabetic, hypertensive and a smoker – perhaps she could call him in for a lifestyle and health check? On further inspection, she discovered he wasn't exactly open to health advice and regularly didn't show for appointments. Perhaps she would need to talk to him face to face. She made a note to add him to her Monday visit.

With nothing left to stall her trip out to her parents, Callie closed down her computer and headed out, checking the road carefully before stepping out of the safety of the surgery. Needless to say, both Steve Miller and Kate thought she had driven straight to her parents' from Kate's house.

It was a sunny day, for once, and the pavements were crowded with weekend visitors making it hard to be sure no one was watching her, so she hurried up the steps to where she had left her hire car parked. Relieved to have got there safely, she drove all the way to her parents, checking her mirrors compulsively, but she saw no signs that she was being followed and it was with a sigh of relief that she finally parked up in front of the large house. Home, at last.

* * *

Callie was already tired of staying at her childhood home by the time she left for work on Monday morning. True to form, her mother had wheedled every detail of her break-up from Billy out of her the night before.

"You should go over there and have it out with the woman. You never know, it might not be anything serious on her part," she said as she poured out more tea for herself and Callie the next morning, picking up where she had left off the night before.

"I'm not going to beg, Mummy."

"Of course not, but you could make sure that you are there and available to pick up the pieces when it all goes horribly wrong."

"And what if it doesn't? What if she is far more suited to being Mrs Iqbal than I ever was?"

That was a question even her mother couldn't answer, but it was all Callie could think about on the drive over to the surgery. Arriving at the car park she used when working, she realised that her parking permit didn't cover the hire car, so she had to pay full cost to leave it for the day. It was not a good start to a Monday morning.

"Good morning," Linda said as Callie passed the reception desk, clutching a takeaway cup of tea and a bag containing a pain au chocolat from the café next door.

"Is it?" she replied.

"I pity your poor patients this morning," the practice manager said to her retreating back.

After her clinic, Callie went up to the office. If she had hoped the pastry would make her feel better, she was disappointed; she felt just as irritated as ever and knew that she had been less than sympathetic with more than one patient.

"Remind me," Linda said, "are you doing visits at the moment or not? Only Mrs Hollis has requested one and you know she only likes to see you."

"I am not going to let this disrupt things any more than necessary," Callie told her, "so I'll do visits."

"Is that wise?" Linda queried.

"Who knows?" Callie answered with a shrug. "But I'm not even in my own car, so it would be hard for anyone to know where I am."

Linda didn't look as if she agreed and, having looked around the office and seen that several eyes and probably even more ears were on this conversation, she led Callie out of the office door.

"Gauri told me you are not thinking of going over to Belfast now," she said quietly.

"No, well, like I told Gauri, it's unlikely. I've withdrawn my application for a post there, so—"

"And are you okay about that?" Linda asked. Callie hesitated before she replied.

"Not really, if I'm honest, but I just have to get on with my life, don't I?" Callie closed the conversation down quickly by going into the doctors' room, where she set about arranging for Violet Osborne to return home, with help from carers three times a day. She was in no mood for anyone to argue with her, as the manager of care services quickly found out. Callie also considered asking

Brian Stenning if he could give a bit of extra support with shopping and such like, but thought she ought to ask Violet first.

* * *

Having left the surgery to do her visits, first port of call was the house where Terence Waldron lived, three doors down from the garden where the bones had been discovered. Callie parked outside his house. The street was slightly set back from the busy main road and she was surprised to find a parking space so easily.

Locking the car, she walked along to see the Mitchells' house. It looked forlorn and abandoned. The forensic tent had gone from the garden, as had the digger, but it didn't look as if there had been any progress with the patio. In fact, the whole garden looked a mess and a piece of police tape tied to a fence post still fluttered forlornly in the wind. She wondered if the Mitchells would ever feel able to return, or if they would sell up. She was pretty sure Mel would be voting to sell, and who could blame her?

Terence, or Terry as he liked to be called, wasn't expecting visitors and certainly not a doctor. He was dressed in stained grey joggers and a T-shirt that had shrunk in the wash and no longer quite covered his beer gut.

"What's this about, Doc?" he asked.

"I just wanted to see that you were okay, Mr Waldron," she replied as he led her through the living room. Unlike the Mitchells' house, there were no patio doors through to the garden, just a window looking out at an unkempt muddle of overgrown bushes, brambles and knee-high grass. Terry was not a gardener, Callie presumed. "You haven't come in for your routine health checks, so I thought I'd come and make sure everything was all right."

Terry didn't question why a busy doctor would take the time to come and see a patient who hadn't asked for a visit and who couldn't even be bothered to look after their own health. In fact, he seemed quite happy with the idea. Perhaps he thought, like Dr Grantham and some television dramas, that a GP popping in to check on a patient was quite normal.

"Yeah, well," he said sitting down. "All the nurse keeps saying is that I need to lose weight and stop smoking, and that's not easy."

"No, I understand that." Callie refrained from repeating the advice, as it was clear that he didn't want to hear it. "Perhaps I can just check your blood pressure and maybe take some bloods while I am here?" She got her stethoscope and some blood tubes out of her bag. "Have you heard any more about the bones they found up the road?" she asked him, nonchalantly.

"Nah," he replied, watching carefully as she placed a blood pressure cuff around his upper arm. "The people there have moved out. I think they're going to sell up."

"Did you know them well?"

"Nah, not really."

"What about the people there before them, the Coopers."

"Nah, well, I met him in the pub a few times, bit of a laugh he was, but they divorced. Moved away."

There was a pause while she checked his blood pressure and then removed the cuff.

"What about before that? The Childses?"

Terry shook his head.

"I tried to keep out of their way when I was growing up."

"Why?" Callie placed a tourniquet round his left arm. "Keep it straight," she told him and started palpating for a vein to take blood from. "Little prick," she warned him.

"Well, he was an angry old sod, 'scuse my French, and she was a bit weird." Terry winced as she took the blood sample. "They had no kids and always complained if I had mates round and we were making too much noise in the garden. A right killjoy he was and I kept out their way."

"Even when you were older?"

"Even more so, she was a bit doolally by then, if you know what I mean. Old Mrs Osborne used to sit with her sometimes because she'd wander."

"And when did you last see them?"

"Is that who they are?" he asked her. "The bones? Are they the Childses then?"

"It's possible, they seem to have disappeared some time ago."

"Yeah," he said suddenly realising why she was there. "You didn't need to take my blood to ask me questions, you could've just asked."

"Yes, but I thought it was too good an opportunity to miss," she told him. "Now, when did you last see the Childses?"

"No idea, I mean, they sold up years ago. Like I told the policeman."

"Yes, but did you see them before the house was sold?" she asked. "In the months leading up to the sale."

He thought long and hard before replying.

"Dunno."

Callie sighed. Terry had been no help at all.

* * *

She got out of the car and grabbed her bag. The patient she was visiting was an elderly lady called Mrs Hollis who lived on her own and whose health had deteriorated in recent months. She had been forced to stop driving because of poor eyesight, much against her will. It was Callie who had been instrumental in the removal of her driving licence when she discovered the old lady couldn't see beyond the bonnet of her car. Callie felt guilty even if she had almost certainly saved someone's life and it meant that she felt obliged to visit when Mrs Hollis needed seeing rather than insist she get a taxi into town.

Callie walked up to the front door, noting that the house was beginning to look in need of painting at the very least, and rang the bell. When there was no response, she opened the key safe, and let herself in.

"Mrs Hollis?" she called out from the doorway. There was the sound of a toilet flushing and then Mrs Hollis, old and bent over a walking frame, came into the hallway and slowly made her way towards Callie.

"Dr Hughes, what a nice surprise, come through," she said as she led the way into the sitting room.

"Can I get you a cup of tea, Dr Hughes?" Mrs Hollis asked, but Callie declined. One of the first things she had learnt when she started going out to do home visits was that you accepted offers of drinks or biscuits at your peril. One look in the kitchens of some households would be enough to put you off food for life.

"What seems to be the problem?" Callie asked her patient once they were both settled in the rose velour three-piece suite and Callie had moved the over-stuffed cushion that took up most of her chair to one side.

"Well, nothing really," the old lady said looking at Callie expectantly. "That's why I was surprised to see you. Do I need another Covid booster or something?"

It wasn't unheard of for elderly patients to forget that they had called for a visit, but Callie had never had any reason to suspect any form of dementia in Mrs Hollis's case.

"The office said you had asked for a visit."

"Really? I'm quite sure I didn't." She looked intently at Callie. "But if they say I did..." She clearly wasn't convinced. "I don't want to get anyone in trouble."

"Well, as I'm here, I may as well just do your blood pressure and–"

There was a sudden bang from outside the house and both Callie and Mrs Hollis jumped at the noise.

"Stay there!" Callie said firmly as she went to look out of the front window.

The hire car was engulfed in flames.

She ran out of the house and looked in amazement. An elderly military-looking gentleman came out of the nearest house, another bungalow a couple of hundred yards away, and hurried towards them.

"Keep back!" he shouted, gesticulating for her to go back in the house. "The petrol tank might blow." He stopped a good distance away and continued to shout. "Keep away from the windows. I've called the fire brigade."

It all seemed like sensible advice and Callie went back inside and ushered Mrs Hollis into the bedroom at the back, just in case there were further explosions while they waited for help to arrive.

* * *

"That's a bit of an ex-vehicle," Jeffries said as they stood looking at the smouldering wreck that had once been her hire car. The fire crew were packing up but said they wouldn't leave for a while in case it burst into flames once more.

"Good job it wasn't my Audi," Callie said. "That's still in the garage being resprayed because of the paint stripper. Did the firemen say why they thought it went up in flames?"

"Molotov cocktail," Jeffries said. "They found the remnants of a bottle under the chassis. Our friend Zac isn't giving up."

"So it would seem," Callie replied. "How on earth do you think he knew where I was?"

"Must've followed you," Jeffries said with a shrug, but Callie didn't think so, she hadn't seen anyone, not that she was trained in how to spot cars following her, but she had seen enough films and had kept a look out for one.

"Mrs Hollis." She nodded towards the old lady who was watching everything going on outside her house from the safety of her lounge. The military man from down the road had joined her. It was probably the most exciting thing to have happened round there in years. "She says she hadn't asked for a visit, so that means whoever did this knew about her, knew that I was always the one to come out to her."

"Or she forgot about calling," Jeffries said. "I mean, she's pretty old."

Callie wasn't convinced.

"You got any more visits to do?" Jeffries asked.

"I called the surgery and the rest are being covered by my colleagues."

"Bet they're not happy about that."

And, of course, they wouldn't be.

"I don't suppose you can give me a lift back to the surgery, can you, Bob? I've promised to do everyone's office stuff to make up for it."

"Least I can do, Doc," he said with a grin and a last look at the car.

The office was full of the news of her car being blown up, and Callie had to try and calm things down by pointing out that it had actually just been set on fire rather than blown up, but it didn't seem to matter.

Linda insisted on making her some hot and disgustingly sweet tea, saying she must be in shock. Callie would have complained but Linda also broke open the chocolate biscuits she kept hidden in her desk. The biscuits were only brought out in dire emergencies such as this, and as they were her favourite plain chocolate digestives, she was grateful. Once everything had settled down, Callie went into the doctors' room to face a very large pile of prescription requests and test results.

The good thing about routine paperwork was that, while it required a certain amount of concentration, most of the thinking was done by the software, telling her the dosages, warning her when a patient was over-ordering, or that two medications clashed, and that meant a part of her mind could think of other things. Like how had Zac, or his accomplice, followed her? She was in a hire car, not her own one, and it had been a last-minute decision to do her own visits, partly because Mrs Hollis had asked for her. Zac couldn't have been sure that she would do visits and Zac couldn't have known that she was always the one to go to that particular patient. Yet, someone *had* known that she would be visiting Mrs Hollis. The trouble was, the more she thought about it, the more she came to the conclusion that it couldn't have been Zac himself.

Much as Callie was fully aware that you never could tell just who was going to turn out to be a criminal, somehow it was too hard to imagine Mrs Hollis working with a disgruntled drug dealer, and also, why would she have allowed the vandalism to have occurred outside her home? If Callie had parked a bit closer to the house, that could have gone up in flames too. It just didn't fit. It had to have been someone who knew Mrs Hollis, or was related to her, who asked for the visit, and who must also know Zac. It was the only explanation that made any sense to her.

Callie pulled up her patients records and checked for next of kin details. A Mr Hollis was listed, but Callie knew for a fact that he had died several years ago, and a quick check confirmed it, so that was no help.

She went through to the main office.

"Linda, who took the call for Mrs Hollis's visit?" she asked.

One of the newer part-time receptionists put up her hand.

"It was me," she said warily.

"And was it Mrs Hollis herself who asked?"

"No, it was her carer."

"She doesn't have carers," Linda said. The poor receptionist bit her lip.

"A man or a woman?" Callie asked.

"It was a man." She was looking more and more anxious as the conversation went on.

"It's okay, you've not done anything wrong, I just need to know how they knew I would be there." She didn't want to badger the poor woman. It was hard enough finding staff without one of them complaining about being bullied.

"He asked for you to visit specifically, said she always saw you, that's why I marked it down like that. I did tell him I couldn't guarantee it would be you, but that I'd try." She looked really miserable.

"That's fine, Carole," Linda told her. "Don't worry about it." She ushered Callie out of the room.

"She needs to know not to take visit requests from anyone but the patient, unless there are exceptional circumstances or the patient has given their permission," Callie said.

"I'm sorry, Callie, I'll have a quiet word with her. You have to remember she's still quite new and we don't want to lose her, she's shaping up to be quite a valued member of staff."

"I know."

"But that does look like that's how he knew you were there."

"Yes, I'll let the police know that's how he knew I would be at the house, but–"

"How did he know about Mrs Hollis and that she only ever saw you?" Linda took the words right out of her mouth.

"Exactly."

Somehow the thought that he knew details like that, about her working life, frightened Callie even more. Zac had infiltrated pretty much every aspect of her life. And if he could do this, it wouldn't be hard for him to find out where she was staying, where her parents lived, or who her friends were. Suddenly, it seemed like everyone in her life was now at risk of becoming collateral damage.

Chapter 21

"I'm worried for my parents' safety," Callie confided to Jayne over the telephone when she called the police station to find out how the investigation was going.

"I don't blame you," she replied. "He certainly seems to know how to track you down. The boss is there now, seeing the old lady."

"I can't help thinking the information about me always visiting her is more likely to have come from someone at the surgery." Callie rubbed at a spot between her eyes, trying to ease the tension that was steadily building. "It's probably inadvertent, you know, just letting something slip." But did she really think that? It would be so much worse to think that someone she worked with was deliberately setting her up, even if that seemed the most likely explanation.

"And we will be speaking to the staff too, especially the lady who actually booked the visit."

"She's the least likely person to have told anyone, isn't she? She's new and after all, why tell us about it if she was setting me up?"

"She may not have known what it was about. Just someone she knows asking about visits and patient details."

"But this is confidential information, she would know that. Every employee is told about the rules. You can't talk about patients or divulge any details outside of work."

"But knowing the rules isn't the same as saying that they never break them, is it?"

Callie had to concede that point. There were always stories going around about nurses accidentally congratulating patients on a pregnancy in the supermarket when the patient's partner doesn't know yet, but this seemed too precise and deliberate.

"I just find it hard to believe that she would own up to taking the call if she was the one who had leaked the information."

"True," Jayne said. "Look, this is a serious crime now, not just some petty vandalism. Someone could have got hurt and everyone working at the surgery will have to be questioned. We can't ignore it."

Whilst it was good to know the police were taking it so seriously, Callie couldn't help feeling there were a lot of people who were going to blame her for the need to go through all this. She just hoped none of them decided to look for other jobs. It was hard enough to keep the surgery fully staffed as it was.

At the end of evening surgery, she asked Linda to call a taxi to take her to her parents' house.

"No need," Linda said and nodded towards a tired-looking Miller, slouched in one of the incredibly uncomfortable chairs by the door, waiting for her.

"What on earth are you doing here?" she asked him.

"Driving you home," he said. "Only way to make sure you get there safely."

"It's very kind of you, Steve, but you can't do your job and be my personal bodyguard."

"I know, and I won't be able to do a taxi run every night, or morning, but just humour me tonight."

She took a deep breath before answering.

"I'll say yes because I'm tired too, and very grateful. Thank you."

They walked out to where his car was illegally parked on double yellow lines. It was a good thing there wasn't much traffic about, because it would have caused a bit of an obstruction otherwise.

She got into the front passenger seat and strapped herself in as he removed the police sign from the front window. It would take a brave, or rather vindictive traffic warden to put a parking ticket on a police car, but she'd seen them ticket an ambulance before now.

"Any news on finding Zac?" she asked when they had set off.

He shook his head. "He seems to have gone deep underground, but we are working on all our sources and I'm hopeful we'll get some news on his whereabouts soon." His face belied his words and Callie felt depressed.

"I worry I'm putting other people at risk," she admitted.

"That's why we wanted you out of the way," he told her. "And honestly? After today, I don't think your parents' house is far enough."

His words mirrored her own thoughts.

"It feels like running away if I take a holiday or something."

"Is that such a bad thing?" he asked. "If it stops someone innocent getting hurt."

"Maybe not, but I've got that hearing into Gerry Brown later this week, so I couldn't go until after that." Even more depressing had been the news from Samuel that Jessica had withdrawn her complaint but the board chair wanted to go ahead with the hearing, with Callie giving evidence about what Jessica had told her. It wasn't as good as having the patient there, but it was the best they could do. Samuel had been apologetic and Callie thought that he, like she herself, believed that Gerry was going to get away with it. Again.

"Anyway, I've managed to wangle a patrol car to be there overnight," Miller continued with a resigned sigh.

"Thank you." She knew just how hard that discussion with the superintendent would have been.

"But I can only promise for tonight, I'll have to see if I can get volunteers after that to cover us until the Gerry Brown thing is over and done with and if we haven't found him by then, you'll just have to go away."

"I can't just go away," she told him.

"Why not?"

"I can't let them down at work."

"They're as worried as I am. It doesn't look good when cars blow up and patients are put at risk."

"But they are also very short staffed, so it's down to you then, to find him before the end of the week and save the NHS." She grinned at him. It was a slightly trembly and tired grin, but a good effort nonetheless. "Consider it an added incentive to find him." Although, she didn't think that Miller needed any added incentive.

* * *

Miller insisted on waiting at Callie's parents' home until the patrol car was in place and parked on the driveway. The wait gave her mother the chance to quiz him on the day's events and ply him with coffee and a home-made fruit cake.

"It's very good of you to go to all this trouble," she told him. "I feel so much safer knowing that there's someone outside the house. I'll take him a flask of coffee and a sandwich before I go to bed."

Callie knew that the chances were high that whoever had drawn the short straw and was on watch tonight would have stocked up on snacks before coming, but her mother was unlikely to listen to her, and anyway, it was a nice gesture.

"And maybe let him use the loo, as well," she suggested. She could see that her mother wasn't so keen on that idea. "Or else he'll have to nip behind a bush."

"Oh dear." Callie's mother pulled a face at the thought.

"I'm sorry I only managed to get the promise of a patrol car for one night," Miller told Callie. "But if they have to leave I'll get a call and from tomorrow, do you think your mother would let me stay?"

"I'm sure she would," Callie said, amazed that he was still prepared to put himself out to this extent. "You'll put on weight, mind, she loves to have someone to feed up."

"Better and better," he replied with a smile that almost reached his eyes.

Once the marked car was in place, Miller left them to go home and get some sleep. She wasn't sure that she would be able to, but in the end was surprised by just how well she did. The security of a police car parked outside the front door worked wonders.

Chapter 22

"Morning, Mummy," Callie called out as she came downstairs, but got no reply. She could hear her mother talking on the telephone in the drawing room so she went into the kitchen where her father was having his breakfast.

"She's letting the neighbours know why there's a police car out front. Doesn't want them thinking we're under house arrest or anything," he explained between mouthfuls of toast and home-made marmalade. If Callie was surprised to see Miller sitting there as well, also eating toast, she hid it well. From the look of him, he hadn't had much sleep.

"Please tell me you didn't spend the night out there in the patrol car," she asked him as she boiled the kettle to make herself some fresh tea.

"No, I was out with Bob, looking for Zac. Just thought I'd drop in and check all was quiet here."

"And have breakfast."

"If it was toast here or a greasy spoon with Bob, which would you choose?"

She didn't need to give that much thought as she put another slice of bread in the toaster.

* * *

Linda told Callie that Gauri, and the rest of her colleagues, had decided it was best if she didn't have any face-to-face contact with patients. No surgeries or visits until the problem with Zac had been sorted, just in case he came in pretending to be a patient. Callie thought they were overreacting, but Linda wasn't going to budge, and handed her a mammoth list of people waiting for a phone call. It was one of the changes that Covid had brought to general practice and not one that Callie liked, and neither did the patients as a general rule. There was no doubt that it did cut down on the number of people needing to come in, but Callie always worried that she would miss something and she knew a lot of patients were put off by having to speak to a doctor by telephone first, particularly if it was something embarrassing. She was sure it was the reason some seemed to delay asking for help. These patients were often the ones that needed to be seen the most.

Callie slowly worked her way down the list and got through a large part of it. Needless to say, Mr Herring, one of the surgery's frequent flyers, had called. With a sigh, Callie rang him back.

"Hello, Mr Herring, it's Dr Hughes here. What seems to be the problem?"

After dealing with several different issues of his, all minor if they existed at all, Callie went to make herself a coffee. She was hungry so she checked the biscuit tin, but there were no whole biscuits left, just a few broken and rather soggy-looking ones.

She went to the office and popped her head round the door. There was no sign of Linda.

"I'm just going to nip next door and get a sandwich," she told the admin assistant, and hurried down to the ground floor and out of the door.

The smell in the café, a mixture of bacon and warm bread, was enough to make her mouth water. She ordered a crab salad sandwich and a flat white to go, and added a home-made chocolate chip cookie to her order at the last minute. Just as she was paying, the door flew open and Linda rushed in.

"What do you think you are doing?" she hissed.

"Getting my lunch," Callie answered calmly, holding up the evidence.

"You know you aren't supposed to leave the surgery alone," Linda continued as she led the way out of the café. Callie hoped no one had heard her, because she didn't want them all wondering what on earth was going on. It was bad enough not being allowed out alone without everyone knowing.

Having reached the end of her call list, and her lunch, Callie had asked two patients to come in for assessment by her colleagues; the rest had required only advice or tests and prescriptions to be ordered. She closed her eyes. There was nothing left of her own work to do, although there were several things she could have offered to do for her colleagues, who were still busy seeing their patients and hers, but she was tired and bored. It was only four thirty, much too early to go home. Perhaps she should go to the police station – by taxi, of course, she could say it was work related then. She would be safe there, wouldn't she? Mind made up, she picked up the phone.

* * *

The CID office was quiet when she arrived. There was no sign of Miller or Jeffries and even Jayne Hales was out. The only person she knew well enough to chat to was Nigel, so he would have to do.

"How's it going?" she asked him as she perched on the end of his desk and looked at the screen he was working on so intently. There was a map of Hastings on it, with a number of pins marking places. "What's that?"

"It's a map of all the cash machines used to withdraw money from Derek Childs' account," he explained.

Callie smiled.

"What?" he asked, suspicious of her amusement.

"The public always seem to think that police work just involves running around arresting people. They never understand that mostly it's about mind-numbingly boring things like watching CCTV recordings or analysing data."

"I don't find them boring," he said, surprised, and she mentally kicked herself. She knew that about Nigel, knew that he found the most tedious of tasks fascinating. She looked again at the maps.

"They're all over the place," she replied. "Hard to work out where whoever was taking the money out lived or worked from this."

"Which makes it all the more likely that it wasn't Mr Childs. I mean, why would he walk all over town to withdraw small amounts of money?"

"True, but it doesn't help us get any clues as to who it was taking the money out, does it?"

"Well, yes, but it does tell us a lot more about what happened." Nigel had a slightly smug look on his face as he clicked on a tab. "I have this fancy bit of software that allows me to colour code the pins according to date or time of withdrawal, amount taken out or whatever else I want." He clicked through a number of pages and Callie began to see patterns emerge.

"Look." He pointed at the map on the screen. "When pensions started to be paid straight into your account, rather than having to be collected from the post office, Derek always took the cash out, the whole pension for both him and his wife, from the machine by the fish and chip shop on a Thursday lunchtime, regular as clockwork."

"Derek was collecting their pensions and getting them a fish and chip lunch every week."

"Exactly. Then, if we look here" – he opened another screen alongside the one he was showing her, which seemed to be Derek Childs' rent details – "he then goes round to the council and pays his rent every week. It all ticks along nicely, until here." He pointed at the screen.

"When there's a large lump sum deposited in his account, in cash."

It was a large sum for that time, indeed. More than thirty thousand pounds.

"Don't the money laundering laws mean it has to be accounted for? You can't just put a large chunk of money like that in without saying where it's come from, I thought."

"Now, yes, but not back then you didn't. So, anyway, the money disappears again here, not long afterwards, which is when he buys the house. Derek no longer has to pay rent, but he still carries on, drawing out their pension in full every Thursday lunchtime."

"Even though they are not paying rent?"

"Yes, they must have been a bit better off. Then pensions started to be paid monthly, but he still drew it all out whenever it was paid in."

"And still from the same cash machine?"

"Yes. And this continues, for years until here." He clicked the mouse again. "A few months before the house was sold he starts using other cash machines, around the town. And then," Nigel continued, "the house is sold and the money goes into the account, here." The smug smile had appeared again.

"It doesn't really help, because we knew most of that, didn't we?"

"Where this really clarifies things, is that, like I said, Derek always withdrew the pensions on the day they were paid in, and only ever withdrew money from the cash machine by the chip shop, but here" – he pointed to the screen – "the withdrawals continue, but in different amounts, sometimes quite large ones, on different days and using different machines. There is no pattern at all."

"You don't think it was Derek taking out the money from then on?" she clarified. If that was the case, it gave them a good indication of when the Childses had died.

"I think it's a logical conclusion."

Jayne came into the room at that moment and dumped her bag on her desk in a way that spoke volumes about her level of frustration.

"Estate agent didn't know anything useful?" Nigel asked her.

"I don't think any of them could have been born when the house was sold," Jayne answered.

"I don't think that's actually–" Nigel started to say but was quelled by a look from Jayne.

"They were at least able to look up their records and give me the name of the solicitor who dealt with it. So I went to see him."

"And?" From the look on Jayne's face, Callie wasn't hopeful.

"He isn't the type to keep staff for more than a few months according to the receptionist. She was busy tidying up her CV and applying for jobs elsewhere while she talked to me. Apparently, he's a bit handsy and a drunk, which I can testify to because when he finally rolled in from his lunch break he absolutely reeked of it."

"Did he remember Derek Childs?"

"Not specifically, no. I doubt that he could remember his own children, to be honest. Why?"

Callie looked at Nigel, who explained.

"I've been looking at the financials and the pattern changes four months before the house was sold to the Coopers."

"Nigel thinks Mr and Mrs Childs may have been killed then," Callie added. It was a bit of a leap, but the best lead that they had so far.

"And therefore, it would have to be someone else pretending to be Derek who sold the house?"

"That's right," Callie answered. "Did they ask for photo ID at the solicitors or the estate agents?"

"No, I did get the receptionist at the solicitors to check the records and they handled both the buying of the house from the council and then the selling of it to the Coopers.

All seems to be in order, but I did notice that there was no photo ID attached, just copies of an old-style paper driving licence, a birth certificate and some utility bills. Could have been anyone who brought them in, although, of course, the money was paid into Derek Childs' bank account."

Callie sighed in dismay.

"Which we already think the killer had access to by this point."

"It had to be someone who knew them well enough to have the bank details," Nigel said.

"Or who was able to torture the information out of them before he killed them," Jayne said morosely.

Callie agreed that it was a very sad scenario, although she knew it happened, not often, but occasionally. Before she had time to say anything, the door to the office flew open and a jubilant Miller burst into the room, followed by a breathless but also grinning Jeffries.

"Got him!" Miller shouted triumphantly.

"Yes!" Jayne punched the air. "Brilliant!"

Callie looked from one to the other, unable to quite understand who they were talking about, but then the penny dropped.

"You found Zac?" Callie was hardly able to believe it might be true.

"Yes!" Miller said. "You're safe. He's not going to be stalking you tonight."

Callie couldn't quite take the news in.

"That's amazing," was all she could find to say. She wanted to hug them, both Miller and Jeffries, but managed to restrain herself.

"Yeah, and he's not going to be out any time soon," Jeffries added.

"Better and better," Jayne said.

"He was found with enough crack to put him away for years," Miller explained.

"That's just, well, um, brilliant," Callie sat down and blinked back some tears of relief that she hoped no one had noticed. Jayne handed her a tissue, so clearly she had. "How did you know where to find him?" she asked.

"Oh, well," Miller looked at Jeffries, who shrugged. "To be honest, we didn't. Got a call from Brighton to say they had raided a suspected drug den and there he was, along with a sizeable haul of crack cocaine."

"Will he say the drugs aren't his, though?" Callie was unable to keep the anxiety from her voice.

"Doesn't matter if he does," Miller assured her, "just being there and not at his mother's was a breach of his bail conditions. He has been recalled to prison with immediate effect." He gave her a reassuring smile. "It's okay, he's not going to be round at yours, damaging things, and if the new charges stick–"

"Which they will," Jeffries interjected.

"He'll get a good few more years as well," Miller said.

Callie was deeply relieved.

"I can go home," she said. "Thank you both so much."

"Don't thank us, thank the Brighton police. All we did was go over there, have a brief, 'no comment' interview with him and add our charges to the sheet."

"Well, I'm still very grateful. Right" – she stood up – "I'm going back to my parents to pick up my things and tell them the good news, and then I'm going home, to put my feet up and relax with a very large glass of wine."

She got almost as far as the door before realising something.

"Oh!" She turned back to where everyone was looking at her and grinning. "I haven't got a car."

* * *

It was Miller who ran her back to her parents' house in the end and waited while she collected her bags and explained the situation to them.

"You know, you don't have to be physically threatened in order to come and visit us," her father told her with a small smile as he helped with the luggage.

156

"I know, Daddy," she said. "I promise I'll come and stay again soon," she told him, but both of them knew she probably wouldn't. "Or we can meet up in town, for a coffee or something. Thank you for being there when I needed you." She hugged her father and then waved goodbye as she got back into Miller's car.

He dropped her at her flat, and it was glorious just to be back home and not to be worrying about who was watching, she realised as she almost skipped up the stairs. To make things even better, the garage had called and left a message to say that her car was ready to be collected. She would go there first thing in the morning on her way to work. Life was back to normal, and it felt good.

She didn't have long to relax and enjoy the peace before Kate arrived with a couple of bottles of champagne, determined to celebrate her friend's liberation.

"We can order in," she announced as the bottle opened with a pop. "Pizza? Chinese? Indian? Or Thai?"

"Anything but Thai," Callie told her. It had been Billy's favourite, and she couldn't face eating it without him yet.

Chapter 23

Callie's head hurt the next morning, so she arranged to pick the car up at lunchtime, just in case she was still over the drink drive limit. She was sure she wouldn't be, she hadn't had *that* much, but her head was definitely a bit groggy and it wasn't worth even the smallest risk. Armed with a large cup of coffee and another pain au chocolat, she was ready to face the day and to give repeated assurances to colleagues that she was back and able to see patients and do visits as normal.

Last patient of the day turned out to be Marcy Draper.

"Good to see you safe and sound, Marcy," Callie said. "I take it you know that Zac's been sent back to prison."

"I heard," she replied as she plonked herself down in the patient's chair. "Bloody good job too, I'd outstayed my welcome at my sister's place."

"What can I do for you?" Callie asked, as if she didn't already know.

"Well, I could do with some pills to tide me over and I want to get back on the methadone programme down here."

As Callie had suspected, Marcy was just trying to get as many drugs as she could out of her doctor. She used the methadone to supplement the stuff she bought, or, Callie thought, to use in a partial trade for the drugs she really wanted – the illegal ones. After a few questions, Callie prescribed a limited amount and agreed to see Marcy again the following week.

"You were okay, were you, Doc? He didn't come after you?" Marcy asked as she was leaving, prescription tightly clasped in her hand.

"He certainly did. He scratched a rude word into my car, poured paint stripper on it and then blew up my replacement car with some kind of Molotov cocktail," Callie replied.

Marcy looked her, open-mouthed with surprise.

"Nah, that don't sound like Zac," Marcy told her. "Scratching a rude word on your car maybe, but he'd probably have signed it with his tag or something to make sure you knew who done it. And the rest? He's much more a fist in your face sort of bloke rather than all that sort of thing. Believe me, if he were really after you, he would have made it up close and personal, made sure you knew who was doing it. None of that squirrelly shit, he ain't got the brains for it."

And with that, Marcy went out, leaving Callie feeling vaguely anxious. It had to be him, didn't it? Who else would have done it? Shaking off the feeling of disquiet she grabbed her visit list and hurried out to collect her car from the body shop.

When she went through the visits scheduled for that afternoon, she was pleased to see that Violet Osborne was on it. She must have finally managed to get discharged from the care home. It would be good to catch up with her and make sure she was getting enough help now she was in her own home.

Callie collected her car and parked in the road outside. There was a 'For Sale' sign outside the Mitchells' house and it still looked empty; perhaps Neil Mitchell had decided to join his wife at the in-laws while they found somewhere else to live. It was sad to think that their forever home had turned out to be such a disaster. Callie didn't think it would be easy to sell the place under the circumstances – although you never could tell. Some buyers might like the macabre history that came with the house.

She went up to Violet's door and rang the bell, calling out as she did so. "It's Dr Hughes and I'm going to let myself in."

She always felt she should warn her patients when she was coming into their home, so that it wasn't a complete surprise but at the same time, she didn't want them to have to get up and open the door unnecessarily. She keyed in the number to open the key safe, took the key and unlocked the door, making sure to replace the key and lock the safe up again before she went into the house.

Violet was sitting in a chair facing the window. Her bad foot was resting on a stool in front of her and her arm was still in a sling, but the plaster had been cut back so that she could at least use her hand.

"Hello, Doctor, thank you so much for visiting me, I do appreciate it. It's just that it's a bit hard for me to get to the surgery at the moment."

Callie had reassured Violet that she was happy to visit and asked about her problem: constipation that was probably caused by the painkillers she was taking. She prescribed some laxatives and asked her what help she was getting from social services.

"I have carers popping in twice a day, to help me get up and go to bed, and meals-on-wheels, so much better than having to cook, so I'm fine. It's amazing what help is available these days, isn't it?"

Callie didn't like to say that she still thought more could be done, and she knew that the carers wouldn't have enough time to stop and chat, or help with anything other than the basics, but it was better than nothing, she supposed. At least it meant that Violet was able to stay in her own home.

"Is there any more news about the skeletons in next doors' garden?" Violet asked. "Were they Derek and Deirdre?"

"It's looking likely, but getting a positive ID isn't really possible."

"Not even with DNA?"

Callie was surprised that her patient knew about such things, but then, she probably watched a lot of crime dramas on TV. Everyone seemed to know about DNA these days.

"There's nothing to compare it to," Callie explained. "So, it can't really help in cases like this."

"I suppose not."

"And they both had false teeth, so dental records are not overly helpful. You don't know of any relatives we could use as a comparison, if they do manage to get a DNA sample, do you?"

"No," Violet shook her head thoughtfully. "The only people I ever saw visit them were that couple that lived down the road in All Saints' Street. Great friends they were. Had two children."

"Derek and Deirdre had two children?"

"No, no, they didn't, the couple who they were friendly with did. The children used to call them Uncle Derek and

Aunt Deirdre, but they weren't really relatives, it was just what we used to do, call people uncle or aunty when they were friends of our parents."

"And they lived in All Saints' Street?"

That's right. What was their name? She used to come and sit with Deirdre if Derek was going out somewhere. Edna, she was. Edna, what was it?" She was lost in thought for a moment. "They both died years ago, of course."

"Oh." Callie was disappointed.

"But the two children would be grown up by now of course." She laughed. "Middle-aged in fact."

"Do you remember their names?"

Violet tried hard to remember, but eventually gave up with a shrug.

"No, I'm sorry."

"Do you know if they still live in All Saints' Street?" Callie asked. "Only it would be helpful to talk to someone who knew the Childses well."

"I think so, I see them around sometimes," Violet said. "But I could be wrong."

"What was their surname, do you know?"

"No." Violet shrugged. "I'm sorry I'm not more help to you."

"You are a great help, believe me. What about Derek and Deirdre, do you remember anything more about them?"

"Not really. They used to keep themselves to themselves. Whenever I tried to talk to her, Derek would intervene. He once called me an interfering old witch after I went to help her bring some washing in when it started to rain. He wasn't a nice man."

"No, I can understand that would make you reluctant to get involved."

"Sometimes you should get involved. Brian and Belinda still used to visit. Even after their parents had died, so they would probably know more about them and where they went."

"Do you remember when you stopped seeing the Childses?" Callie asked her. "Was it before the house was sold."

"Now you're asking." Violet laughed. "It was a long time ago." She thought some more. "Actually, I am sure they had left before the house was sold. A big van came and took all their furniture, Brian helped the men load it all up, and then he showed the estate agents round when they came. He told me that Derek and Deirdre had gone into a home and he was helping them out. I remember because he was quite short with me when I asked where they had gone. He told me to mind my own business. I wasn't being nosy," she said, "I just wanted to know that Deirdre was all right because sometimes, you know, Derek wasn't very kind to her."

"I'm sure you meant well." Callie stood up to leave. "If you do remember any more about Belinda and her brother, like their surname or where they live, please let me know."

"Of course, Doctor," Violet reassured her. "I'm sure it will come to me, eventually."

Callie smiled and went to leave but turned back at the door.

"Oh, I meant to suggest, if you need any errands done, there's a local man who I could ask to help out. So let me know if you want me to get in touch with him."

She waved as she went out, thinking about how she could search for a brother and sister, names and dates of births not known, who maybe lived in All Saints' Street. She could check patient records, of course, and ask Nigel to help, but given how little detail they had, she wasn't hopeful that either of them would be successful.

Chapter 24

Callie wandered into the office.

"You haven't forgotten I'm out tomorrow, have you?" she asked Linda.

"As if we could forget," she replied. "And what about you, are you all prepared?"

"As prepared as I'll ever be."

A telephone rang and one of the admin assistants answered it before waving the receiver at Callie.

"It's for you, Dr Hughes. Mrs Osborne, do you want her notes up on screen?"

"No that's fine, I can get them if I need them" Callie answered as she took the receiver. "Hello, Violet, what can I do for you?"

"It came to me, just now, Dr Hughes. They were called Stenning, Edna and Tom."

It took a moment or two for Callie to remember what the question was that Violet was answering.

"The married couple who were friends with the Childses?"

"That's right, he was a bit of a bully, I always thought. Not unlike Derek in some ways. But the children were much less so, quiet and unassuming. Derek got on well with the boy, used to call him the son he never had. I always thought that was rather sad, but Deirdre would never have been able to look after a child, she was too much like one herself, and I wouldn't have wanted any child to have a father like Derek."

"Funnily enough, it was a Brian Stenning I was going to suggest to help you if you needed anything. I know he does some shopping and bits for others in your area. Could that be the son?"

"Brian, yes, I remember now. Brian and… and… Oh, what was her name? Thin, anxious girl, let me think, Barbara? No, Belinda, that's it, Belinda and Brian."

Callie checked the surgery details, quickly got an address for the Stennings and rang Nigel.

"Hi, Nigel, it's Callie here," she said. "Belinda and Brian Stenning are local people who knew the Childses well growing up. They may be able to help give us more details about the time they went missing."

There was some clicking sounds as Nigel put their details into his computer.

"Do they live at Rose Cottage, All Saints' Street?" he asked.

"That's right," she said. "Violet Osborne had a flash of inspiration and remembered their names."

"Brilliant," he said. "I'll let Jayne know as soon as she's back and arrange for someone to go and interview them."

"Can't you go? This might be the breakthrough we need." Callie was impatient, after all this time trying to identify the bones and find out how they came to be buried in the back garden, maybe, at last they would know.

There were a few moments of silence. "There's no one here at the moment," Nigel explained. "And I can't really leave the office…"

Callie was frustrated that there would be a delay. "I can pop in and see them if that helps? Find out if they know anything about our mystery bones." Callie felt she was on a roll and didn't want to lose momentum. She desperately wanted to find out more.

"I'm not sure–" Nigel began.

"It's no trouble and I just want to ask them if they know where the Childses are and if they are still alive. I know someone will have to get a formal statement at a later point."

"I really don't think you should, Dr Hughes." Nigel sounded anxious. "I'm sure it can wait until someone gets back here," he said. "You won't go on your own, will you?"

"Of course not," Callie said, to put his mind at rest, even though she had no intention of doing as she said, after all, she had found the lead and she wanted to follow it up herself.

* * *

Brian and Belinda Stenning lived in a small, terraced house on All Saints' Street, presumably the same house their parents had lived in and not a cottage at all, Callie couldn't see any roses, either. She had passed it many times on her way to The Stag, but never really noticed it. The house was in dire need of doing up. The curtains drawn across the grubby windows were missing hooks, so they sagged in places. Looking up she could see that there was more than a tile or two missing from the mossy roof. The damp and shady front garden had been badly concreted over at some point, and weeds poked through the cracks, while bits of rubbish that had blown in were strewn around the area.

A laminated sign had been stuck to the door saying 'No hawkers, free papers or flyers' – at any rate, she thought that was what it said. It was hard to read through the curled and yellowed Sellotape.

She rang the bell and waited; at least that seemed to be in working order, as she had heard it ring. Glancing to her right, she was pretty sure the curtain had twitched in response to the doorbell, but there was no answer, so she rang again. She was tempted to peer through the letter box, but that had been taped shut too. Moving closer to the door, she could hear quiet whispering going on in the hallway but the voices were too quiet for her to be able to hear what was being said.

"Mr Stenning?" she called through the door. "It's Dr Hughes. I just want to ask you some questions about some people you knew? Derek and Deirdre Childs?"

After some more whispering, Callie heard some bolts being drawn, the rattle of a chain and a key turned in the lock. Eventually, the door opened a fraction and a pointy, weaselly face appeared, eyes wide with fear, or anxiety. Or both.

"Yes?" the woman said, with a slight quaver in her voice.

"My name is Dr Hughes, are you Miss Stenning? Belinda?" Callie tried smiling reassuringly.

"Betty," she said. "I go by the name Betty. Like Betty Grable."

Callie couldn't imagine anyone less like Betty Grable. She could make out a bulkier figure in the gloom of the hallway.

"Is Mr Stenning here?"

"Ask her in, Betty." A voice came out from the hall, and Betty reluctantly held the door open for Callie to enter.

Callie walked down the hallway which was covered in framed, black-and-white photographs from a bygone age. She stopped to look at them.

"Hello, Dr Hughes," Brian said and he nodded towards the pictures. "I deal in Hollywood memorabilia," He was wearing a dress shirt buttoned to the neck, with a Fair Isle tank top over it. His pale blue eyes looked at her from behind his glasses with an intensity she found unsettling.

"We both do," Betty corrected him.

He turned his gaze to his sister and nodded.

Callie was shown into the sitting room and Brian quickly removed a box from the sofa so that she could sit down. He and Betty sat on dining chairs he pulled out from the completely covered dining table. There were boxes everywhere except on the table set against one wall, where a desk-top computer was positioned, along with a printer and other peripherals.

"We've got Marlon Brando's T-shirt from *On the Waterfront*," Betty told her. "Signed and everything."

"And Steve McQueen's leather jacket from *The Great Escape*," Brian added with pride. "Fully authenticated."

"Amazing," Callie replied, not sure if she believed it. "Have you done this for long?"

"Yes, I gave up work ten or fifteen years ago to do it full time because I was so successful," he said.

Callie resisted the temptation to look pointedly at the cheap shabby furniture and call him out on that.

"So, the Childses? I understand you knew them very well."

"Yes, yes, we did." He seemed curiously reluctant to say more. "Do forgive me, where are my manners? Would you like a cup of tea?"

"No, it's fine, thank you," she assured him. "The Childses?" she prompted. "Do you know where they went?"

"Somewhere up north, wasn't it, Betty?" He looked at his sister who panicked slightly.

"I don't know," she said. "Maybe?"

"When was that?" Callie asked.

"Now you're asking," he replied. "I really don't remember."

"But you helped sell the house? Showed the estate agent round?"

"No," he said firmly. "You've got that wrong. We stopped seeing them before then."

"Long before." Betty nodded her agreement.

"And you helped the removal men, when they came to collect the furniture," she persisted.

"No," he said and pursed his lips, no longer so friendly. "Someone's been telling you lies. Someone is trying to get me into trouble." He stood up. "I think you should go now."

Callie was surprised by the sudden change in his demeanour, but she knew that she had no legal right to be there and so had little choice but to do as she was asked and go.

* * *

Back at the police station, Callie told Jayne and Nigel about her encounter.

"You really shouldn't have done that," Jayne told her, and Callie knew she was right. Nigel looked worried that she might take it out on him, or worse, tell the boss that he'd helped Callie, even if he hadn't, but Jayne simply gave him a reproachful look. She knew Callie could be impulsive and it was hard to stop her when she was determined.

"Anything could have happened," Jayne said with an exasperated shake of her head.

"A neighbour told me that he showed the estate agent round and helped the removal men. He must know where they went, if, indeed they went anywhere, even if he denies it now," Callie insisted.

"If your patient has remembered it right," Jayne said. "It was a long time ago and her memory might not be as good."

"I'm sure she does, it's the short-term memory that tends to go, old people remember the past as clear as day."

Jayne sighed. "If this Brian and Belinda are involved, your visit will have worried them. I had better get some uniforms to pick them up as quickly as possible."

"Sorry," Callie said. She was beginning to see that her visit might have complicated matters. "Hopefully it will mean they want to help clear things up."

"Or they might just refuse to talk to us," Jayne countered.

"And if they do that?"

Jayne shrugged.

"We'll cross that bridge when we come to it."

"The other thing," Callie admitted, "is that Brian often does errands for other old people around town. Shopping, getting out cash out for them and so on. If he was pocketing money from Derek and Deirdre, I'm beginning to worry that he might be helping himself to cash from them too."

"People trust him with their PIN numbers?"

"How else can he get cash out for them? I know it's inadvisable, but what else are the elderly and disabled supposed to do?"

Nigel had been tapping away at his computer as they talked.

"The Stennings jointly own the house in All Saints' Street, although there's a hefty mortgage on it," he said.

"So they can't just up and leave," Callie told Jayne, hoping it was true.

"If they're scared enough, they might." Jayne turned back to Nigel. "Have you asked the bank to cancel the cards and freeze the Childses' accounts?"

"I'll get onto that right away," he told her and hurriedly focused on his computer.

"Wouldn't it be better to leave it open?" Callie asked. "I mean, is the account still being used?"

"Yes," Nigel looked at the screen in front of him. "Fifty pounds was taken out last week. We got the photo of whoever was using it, but it's not much use."

He brought the pictures up to show her, and she had to agree. The person using the machine was looking down the whole time, wearing a mask and had a baseball cap pulled low. Cursing Covid and the fact that wearing a mask was no longer seen as strange, she tried to see if there were any features she could make out, but there weren't. She couldn't even tell if it was a man or a woman.

"I take your point," she agreed sadly. "Is there still money in the account?"

"More than five thousand pounds."

"Wouldn't it be useful to leave it open and get alerts when it's used, faster than you're getting now, if it's possible. Maybe you could even stake out some favourite bank machines and wait to see who is using it."

"Possibly," Jayne said, but Callie could tell she wasn't convinced. "Are there any favourites?" she asked Nigel.

"Not really, they've used twenty different ones along the coast in the last few months."

"I don't think we have the manpower to watch them all," Jayne told Callie, and she had to agree. It would take too long and need too many people to be feasible. "But maybe we could see if the banks can give us rapid feedback on when the card is used. That would at least give us a chance."

"I'll talk to them," Nigel said. "But I don't think they'll be able to do it fast enough for us to get a patrol car there in time."

"Still," Jayne said, "we can try. And I'll talk to the boss about what else we can do."

Callie knew she would have to be happy with that.

Chapter 25

Callie met Kate in The Stag after they had both finished work. She had walked past the Stenning house, hoping to see one or the other of the occupants, but the house seemed quiet. A light from an upstairs window gave her hope that they hadn't done a runner, at least.

Despite the coolness of the evening, it was dry and Callie had found a table in the garden as the bar was over-crowded. She was sitting there when Kate arrived and looked at Callie's glass of fizzy water with disdain.

"What?" Callie said with a laugh. "I need to keep a clear head to give evidence tomorrow."

"God, yes. Here's to a successful outcome." Kate raised her own pint of beer in a toast and clinked with Callie's glass.

"I don't suppose you've heard from Samuel about whether Jessica has changed her mind again and is willing to give evidence now?" Callie asked.

Kate shook her head. "Samuel said they are waiting to see if she turns up before making a decision as to whether or not to go forward if she doesn't. So, if she isn't there and they do still agree to hear the case, it's down to you to make it stick."

Before they could talk more, Callie's phone rang and she saw that it was Jayne. Looking round to make sure there was no one else in the garden with them, and seeing that there wasn't, Callie answered the call.

"Hi, Jayne," she said and was surprised to hear, huffing and puffing from the other end of the line and some muffled shouts. "Is everything all right?"

"They're on the move," Jayne managed to say between breaths.

"Who is?"

"Whoever is using the bank card," she replied, and Callie heard the sound of a car door slamming and the engine starting. "I called the Stennings and left a message saying that we wanted to interview them in the morning. Shortly afterwards, the card was used, taking out the maximum amount allowed." Jayne's voice was steadier now as she was presumably being driven.

"You think they are doing a runner?"

"Definitely. Someone tried to use the card again in Ashford a couple of hours later, but it wouldn't give them anything because they'd already had the daily maximum."

"Ashford?"

"Yes, Brian Stenning has a car according to the DVLA, so we're hoping it will ping a camera. We've put out an all-ports alert, particularly Dover and the tunnel, although they could be heading for London–" there was some speaking in the background and Callie heard the words 'hit' and 'A20'. "Okay, we've had an ANPR alert on the car, it looks like they're heading to Dover. I'll let you know what happens later." Jayne ended the call.

"Did you get all that?" Callie asked Kate who had moved closer so that she could hear more of what was going on.

"Pretty much. This is the couple that knew the people who you think the bones belong to, is it?"

"That's right, I'm pretty sure they're involved in some way, stealing their money at the very least even if they didn't actually kill them."

"But why on earth would they rabbit like that?"

"Because I went to see them and they wouldn't talk to me, so I got Jayne to call and she left a message asking them to come in for interview tomorrow morning."

"They must have very guilty consciences if they decided to run rather than stay and deny everything, or better still just no comment their way through every interview."

"That's the defence solicitor in you saying that. Most people would be a bit freaked out by an official interview, and they may think the police have more evidence than they do."

Kate looked at her empty glass.

"Come on, have a proper drink, it's going to be a long wait and I really want to hear the outcome."

Callie weakened and ordered a glass of Pinot Grigio. Kate was right; it was going to be a long night.

* * *

Rather than get too drunk, given that Callie had to be in London the next day for the hearing, they went to Kate's house after a couple of drinks, and Callie moved on to drinking tea after eating the fish and chips they had picked up on the way. It was almost eleven by the time Jayne rang again and by then Callie's nerves were in shreds.

"We got them," Jayne said triumphantly. "They were stopped by the border police at Dover."

"Brian and Belinda?"

"Yes, both of them, and the car was absolutely packed to the gills. It looked like they intended to stay away for a long time."

"Are you bringing them back for questioning?"

"Yes, we actually had to arrest them, as they weren't going to come back voluntarily."

"What did you arrest them for? Murder?"

"No, theft. He had Derek Childs' bank card in his wallet as well as a couple of others with different names on. It's really the only solid proof we have of anything, and arresting them means the clock is ticking, so I'll have to go. Bye!"

Callie hardly had time to thank Jayne for letting her know what was happening before she hung up, keen to get the two suspects back to Hastings as quickly as possible.

"Have they got enough to charge them with theft do you think?" Callie asked Kate.

"If they had a bank card in Childs' name on them, that's a given, I should think. Unless Brian can produce your man Derek and show that he gave permission for them to use it."

"But as we think he's dead and buried, he can't do that."

"No, dead men might tell no tales, but they can't give you permission to take their money either."

"Quite," Callie said. "It's good to know that Steve will at least be able to ask them about the bones. I suspect one of them will talk if he pushes them."

"We can only hope. And speaking of which, I'm glad I'm not on call as duty solicitor tonight. I would have to advise no comment and that would make you cross." Kate couldn't keep a slight note of regret from her voice; a high-profile case like this would certainly help raise her profile.

"Of course it wouldn't make me cross," Callie lied. "I know it's your job and everyone is entitled to the best defence they can get, but I am very glad that means they won't get you, and a bit of me hopes they aren't clever enough to ask for any legal representation at all." She looked at her watch and yawned. "Anyway, I'd best get back home so that I can get my beauty sleep. There won't be any more news tonight."

Callie headed along the road rather than the faster route up the steps and across the country park. Even with a torch, she didn't feel safe walking across the large, unlit expanse towards her home anymore, she had seen far too many horror movies to risk anything as silly as that. At least the road had streetlights and houses all the way to hers even though it was a longer route and meant that she had to zig-zag up the hill back to her flat. Besides, she told herself, there would be fewer rabbit holes to trip her up.

* * *

She was with that bitch again, but then left the place alone. I was worried that she would stay the night there and go straight to the hearing in the morning, but I didn't think she was going to do that. She hadn't taken a bag or anything that might hold a change of clothes with her from the pub, so she was most likely planning to walk home. So here I am waiting for her to come home. Her car is still in its place, outside her house, parked exactly where I'd already targeted it. I thought about waiting at the cliff top, but then I was worried she might walk back along the road rather than that way. It is safer to wait here, hidden behind her car and the wheelie bins again. It is such a good hiding place as I wait for her to come to me. I know she is on her way, it won't be long now. I have filled a plastic spray container with acid in readiness, and this time, I'm not going to waste it on the car.

Chapter 26

As she walked along the road, Callie could see the house up ahead of her. Her car was in its usual position parked by the bins. Not the safest of places, but there were few houses with garages or even driveways in the Old Town and she was very lucky to have a parking spot at all.

The light was on over her front door, but the house was beyond the last street light and there were no lights on in any of the flats. Mrs Drysdale would have gone to bed and Howard, the middle-aged rocker in the middle flat, was probably still out on the town, doing whatever middle-aged rockers did at night.

As she passed under the last streetlight, she fished around in her handbag for her keys. She knew she had thrown them in the main compartment rather than in one of the side pockets and she had to rummage around a bit to find them again. As she finally felt them and pulled them out, something fell from her bag. She stopped to pick it up. It was a small plastic disc, about the size of a poker chip. She walked back so that she was directly under the street lamp and held it up, but there wasn't enough light to see clearly. She groped around in her bag again and felt for her torch and clicked it on. It was bright enough for her to be able to inspect the object more closely in its light. The disc wasn't something she had ever seen before and it certainly wasn't something that belonged to her. There was a logo on it that suggested it was something to do with her phone. She wondered what it was doing in her bag. She took a photo of it and sent it to Kate with a message asking if it was hers and asked if it had maybe got into Callie's handbag by mistake.

That done she started walking towards her flat again. Just as she got close her phone started ringing and she took the call.

"Hi, Kate, is that disc thing yours?" she asked.

"It's a smart tag," Kate said anxiously. "It's used to track objects, and unfortunately these days, people."

Callie stopped.

"You think someone has been tracking me?" Callie took a moment to digest what she was saying, "It would explain how Zac knew where I–"

She broke off at the sound of a movement to her right.

"What's going on?" Kate asked.

"Probably just a fox," Callie tried to reassure her, and herself, but the hairs were standing up on the back of her neck as she stared into the gloom, looking for any further movement. There was nothing. Callie crossed over the road, away from the bins and her car, so that she was on the side of the road where her front door was only a few short steps away. Keys in one hand, phone in the other, she rushed towards the door and the safety of her home.

There was a crash as one of the bins was thrown heavily to one side and someone rushed out from behind them and ran towards her. Whoever it was, he was dressed all in black, including a balaclava covering most of his face.

"What!" Callie had time to shout before she was aware of a stinging sensation on her cheek, she closed her eyes and turned away.

"Bitch!" a voice shouted and she dropped her phone.

"Help!" Callie called as she ran for her door, keys still in her hand. "Help!" Hoping Kate, or someone nearby, could hear. Someone other than her attacker, that was.

Whoever had sprayed her with acid, and she was pretty sure from the pain she was feeling that that was what it was, was still chasing her, spraying at her head. She turned, with her eyes closed, and swung at him, keys still in her hand, and connected with his face.

"Fuck!" he shouted. When she opened her eyes he was clutching his face, blood pouring down the hands that were covering his eyes. He had dropped the spray, and Callie kicked the bottle away and then kicked him for good measure.

"You've fucking blinded me, you fucking bitch!" the attacker said, still holding his damaged face. Something about the angry way he spoke triggered a memory, but she didn't wait around for it to clarify; she opened her front door, rushed inside and slammed it shut behind her. She ran up the stairs two at a time and once inside her flat, ran straight into the bathroom, turning the shower full on and climbing into the bath, fully dressed. She turned her face up, to let the water fall on it, opening her eyes to make sure that they too were washed clean. She was drenched in seconds, but she kept the water full on, as she crouched, crying under the water.

* * *

176

There were, once again, blue flashing lights outside her window as Callie sat on the sofa next to Kate and a paramedic shone a light into her eyes.

"Are they sore at all?" he asked.

"No, I think I managed to turn away and keep the acid out of them, and then I made sure I washed them out in the shower," she told him.

"Good job," he said, which, she thought, was the understatement of the year. She shivered at the thought of what might have happened if the acid had got into her eyes.

"You must be cold," Kate said. "Perhaps you should get out of your wet things."

Callie was wrapped in her towelling bathrobe, but still had most of her wet clothes on underneath. Her soaking wet hair was wrapped in a towel.

"Yeah, I want to check for skin burns, as well," the paramedic said. The room felt full, with the paramedic and his co-worker, a uniformed police officer, and Kate.

A second policeman arrived and shook his head.

"Has he got away?" Callie asked, slightly hysterical. "Please don't tell me he has."

"We'll get him, Doc, don't you worry." But he didn't manage to convey much hope in his words.

"Perhaps if we go in the bedroom?" Kate suggested. "Get you out of these things and let this nice young man look at your injuries." She was being gentle and kind and Callie couldn't bear it. She started to cry again. At that moment, of course, Miller came rushing into the room, closely followed, as ever, by Bob Jeffries.

"Oh my God!" he said and hurried to her, making as if to give her a hug, but she flinched away. "Are you okay?" he asked.

"I thought you said Zac was safely locked up," Kate told him angrily.

"He is," Miller replied. "It can't have been him."

"Who else could it have been?" Kate responded.

"It wasn't Zac," Callie sniffed and told them, suddenly very sure of who it was, "it was Gerry, Gerry Brown. I recognised his voice. He's been tracking me everywhere I go. He must have put that thing in my bag when he confronted me at the surgery."

"Are you sure?" Miller asked.

"Yes!" She was trying to sound calm, but she could hear that her voice was just edging towards hysteria.

"Right," Miller said and turned to Jeffries. "Let's go and pick him up."

Taking a deep breath to keep herself under control, Callie turned and called out to his retreating back, "I'd try the hospital as your first port of call. I think I got him in the eye with my keys." She looked pointedly at the bloodstained set of keys on the table.

"Good job," said Kate and Miller nodded.

"Bag 'em up," he instructed Jeffries.

As Jeffries donned gloves and placed the keys in an evidence bag, one of the other policemen chimed in with, "There's quite a lot of his blood outside for DNA, as well."

"Every little thing helps nail the bastard," Jeffries said. "Point it out to the CSIs when they get here."

* * *

Much later, when Callie had convinced the paramedic that her acid burns were largely superficial thanks to the quick and liberal application of water and had persuaded him to let her stay at home, she sat nursing a cup of warm milk and talking to Kate as they waited to hear whether Miller had found Gerry Brown.

"He was waiting behind the bins," Callie said to her friend.

"I know," Kate said soothingly. "I heard it all, remember?" And despite herself, she shivered.

"I'm sorry, it must have been tough hearing me being attacked like that."

"What was tough, was keeping on listening as I dialled 999 on my landline and told them what was going on. I wanted to rush straight up and kick him where it hurts, if I'm honest, but knew I needed to get help, rather than just arrive, a breathless, sweaty mess too late to be any use at all."

Callie smiled as she thought about Kate rushing up the hill to come to her rescue.

"And then when I do arrive, before the ruddy police, I might add, I find no one there but a puddle of blood on your doorstep and the door firmly closed. I rang and rang, but–"

"I was in the shower."

"I know that now, but at that time I thought you must have been abducted, so I rang all the bells and woke Mrs Drysdale up. I'm sorry."

"Was she very cross?"

"I didn't stop to find out, just rushed up the stairs to your place, the door was wide open and then, well, you know what then, you were sitting in the bath with the shower full on and crying."

Which, of course, she had been.

"I was so relieved to see you, but then I saw some of the burns on your head and neck."

"Are they very bad?"

"Have you not looked at them?"

"Not really, only the ones on the front of my neck, the paramedic said they were the worst–"

"Yes, although there are some on your head–"

Callie instinctively reached up.

"No, don't touch them," Kate ordered. "They are all covered in that gunk the paramedic put on."

"Not exactly looking my best then?"

"No, but he didn't seem to think there would be any permanent damage, did he?"

"A bit of scarring, maybe, but not too bad. I'll know more when they start to heal. I just hope my hair covers the worst of it."

Callie didn't want to think about it anymore; she didn't want to worry about being scarred for life, or having bald patches where the skin never recovered. She shuddered again and curled up into a foetal position right there on the sofa, but not before placing a towel under her head, to stop the gunk getting on the cushions.

"I'm so tired," she said.

"Well, try and sleep," Kate said. "I'll stay here and watch over you." And she did.

Epilogue

Callie watched from the window as the two men carried a heavy, chintz-covered sofa and loaded it into the removal van that was completely blocking the lane. As the last house on the road, there was no problem with them doing that, although she would not be able to get her car out until they had left. But she wasn't going anywhere. She wasn't back at work yet, and she didn't feel up to it just yet anyway. She was so tired. She didn't have the energy to do much, and she didn't think they would be loading the van for much longer as it was almost completely packed and Mrs Drysdale would be gone soon too.

She wondered if she should go out there and speak to the men before they left. After all, she was going to need someone to move her own things out in a few weeks' time.

There had been plenty of time for thinking in the days since the attack and she had finally come to the conclusion that whilst her penthouse home was lovely, as well as secluded and quiet, both things she had thought of as advantages, in the light of recent events she had changed her mind. She needed somewhere more in the centre of town, for her own safety as much as her neighbours'. She wanted light, noise and, more than anything else, people around her.

Someone to hear when she screamed for help, and better still, someone who would help her when she did.

She had tried to explain to Mrs Drysdale that as she was planning on leaving, for a while at least, her neighbour shouldn't feel that she had to be the one to go, but her mind, and the mind of her son, had already been made up. Mrs Drysdale was not staying in her flat a moment longer than she had to, not after all that had happened. Her son had found her a nice apartment in a sheltered facility for the elderly. It didn't have such nice views, but it did have a warden and she would feel safe there. Callie could understand that point of view. After all, safety was exactly what she was looking for as well.

At last, the removal men closed the van doors, went around to the front, climbed into the cab and drove away. She had missed the chance to speak to them, lost the opportunity to ask about her own move, too tired of it all to move from her seat by the window. She supposed this lethargy was a reaction to all that had happened in the last few days, that perhaps she could even be depressed, but she didn't think so. She mentally shrugged. She could call the removal firm later, when she was ready.

She watched as Mrs Drysdale came out of the front door, accompanied by her son. The old lady turned and took a long last look at the building where she had lived for twenty years before she was driven out by the problems caused by Callie. Callie finally stood up and raised a hand of apology as the son glared up at her. She didn't mind, she could understand how he must feel about the danger she had brought to his mother's home. If she were him she would be angry and if she were Mrs Drysdale, she would have left too.

Callie knew she was right to move now, and not just because of fear. The flat had too many memories of Billy: the spices in the cupboard for when he used to cook for her, the razor in the bathroom. She could blitz the place and remove every trace of him, but she couldn't get rid of the memories of him laughing at her jokes, of him making love to her, or of him bleeding from the near fatal stab wound that had been meant for her.

Jayne had visited and told her about the interviews with Brian and Belinda, who still insisted that she wanted to be called Betty.

"It was her that broke first, tripping over her words in her need to get her story across. He just sat there smiling smugly and saying 'no comment'."

Callie could believe that. He had been the stronger of the two.

"But when he heard she had talked to us, he decided to tell his side of the story too."

"What did happen to the Childses?" Callie asked her.

"It all goes back to the Stenning parents, Edna and Tom. It seems that Tom was best mates with Derek and kept telling him he ought to buy his council house, you know, when they were handing out huge incentives for people to do that."

"The Thatcher years."

"Exactly. But Derek didn't have the money, so his mate, Thomas Stenning, lent him the money to do it.

"Wow!"

"On the condition that he pay rent to the Stennings, just as he had to the council, and that he make a will signing the house over to them or to the two young Stennings when he and Deirdre died."

"So the house really belonged to Brian and Betty?"

"Not until the Childses were dead and they couldn't claim it because they couldn't admit that they were dead. That's why Brian had to pretend to be Derek with the solicitors and estate agents."

"He had access to their accounts? How did he get the pin number?" Callie hoped they hadn't forced it out of him.

"Just like you said. It seems that when Derek got too old to go himself, Betty used to go and collect their fish and chips and get the pensions out of the machine for them. That way Brian and her could subtract the rent at the same time. It was a neat set-up."

"Then what went wrong?" Callie asked.

"Derek couldn't cope with Deirdre at home. He wanted them both to go into a care home, and wanted it to be a nice one."

"And the only way to do that was to sell the house." Callie was beginning to understand what had happened.

"That's right," Jayne said. "You should have heard the anger in Brian's voice when he told me about that. He said it wasn't Derek's house it was theirs. It was their legacy, left to them by their parents, so Derek couldn't sell it to pay for care. Unfortunately, Derek pointed out that it was his name on the deeds and he'd destroyed the will that left the house to Brian and Betty."

"And that didn't go down well?"

"Not well at all, but their stories diverge here, with both of them blaming the other. Betty says Brian pushed Derek and he fell and hit his head, and Brian says the same except that it was Betty who pushed him. The result was the same."

"A dead Derek," Callie said.

"And a Deirdre who had slept through it all. One of them, and they both blame the other again, held a pillow over her face until she stopped breathing."

"I hope it was quick and she didn't know what was going on."

"So do I," Jayne agreed.

"And then they buried them in the garden?" Callie asked.

"Yes, in the middle of the night and they put an old tarpaulin and some broken bits of wood over the place so no one would see that it had been dug up."

"That must have been hard work, even with the two of them doing it, all that digging and moving bodies."

"They were younger then, of course – it was nearly twenty years ago."

"Of course." Callie knew she was right. "And then they sold the house and no one questioned where the Childses had gone. And having access to the house money meant Brian could give up his job and deal in Hollywood memorabilia."

"Except most of the stuff they had was fake." Jayne shook her head in disbelief. "I mean buying all that stuff on eBay? It was never going to be real, was it?"

"Oh dear, not fully authenticated, then?" Callie smiled at the thought of them being conned like that.

"No. Oh there were a few autographs and things the experts said might be real, but none of the big stuff, the expensive items, were. And anyway, how can you be a dealer when you never sell anything. You're just a collector."

"Or an enthusiast, I think they're called." Callie thought for a moment. "Why did no one miss the Childses?"

"I think it helped that no one had actually liked them, so no one was sorry that they'd gone."

"Their only friend, Mr Stenning senior, had already died," Callie added, thinking how sad that was.

She thought about it as she sat looking out of the window long after Jayne had gone. Wondered who would miss her and being surprised by the list. Her parents, Kate, Steve Miller, even Bob Jeffries – and that was before she even got onto her work colleagues. Although some wouldn't miss her personally, they'd miss the work she usually did. But Linda would miss her, she thought. Lots of people would miss Brian Stenning now he was under arrest. Who was going to shop for the elderly? Collect their pensions for them? Rob them blind?

It was Linda who had told her about one of the flats above the surgery that was for rent. She had suggested that Callie should take it and rent her own flat out. It would give her time to think about whether or not she wanted a more permanent move and she would only have to climb two flights of stairs to reach her home at the end of a working day. Right now, even that seemed too much but she had gone to look at it and taken it on the spot. It was the flat on the top floor and there was a balcony and although the view was partially blocked by the dark looming net sheds, she definitely could see the sea. Not as good a view of it as she had from up here, but a sea view, nonetheless. It would have to do and it would be good to be so close to the sea, even if there would also be the smell of fish from the shops and stalls along the road and the net sheds, but she could cope with that. She could cope with a lot to feel safe, she decided.

As she stood at the window, long after Mrs Drysdale and her son had left, she saw Steve Miller walk up the road. He must have left his car further back, where the road was wider. She smiled to herself and went to the kitchen to put the kettle on.

It would be good to hear his news.

She knew that Gerry Brown had been found in the A&E department of Brighton hospital the night of the attack on her. He had given a false name and insisted he had been in an accident in his garage, but the hospital staff had been put on the alert to report any injuries of this nature and thankfully they did. He was arrested in the hospital, soon after he had got out of the operating theatre, and before he had had time to discharge himself.

She couldn't find it in her to feel satisfaction, or even horror, that he had had to have his badly damaged left eye removed. After all, he had brought it on himself, she thought, although she was glad her keys were being kept as evidence. She really didn't want to have them back. Her hand crept up to her head, to the scabby patches where the burns were healing fast, but not as fast as she would have liked. She was still very self-conscious about how she looked.

When the door buzzer went, Callie let Miller in and then went back to the kitchen area and poured boiling water onto the ground coffee she had spooned into a cafetière. She had plenty of fresh milk these days; every visitor seemed to bring some with them, along with packets of biscuits, knowing that she wasn't going out shopping just yet. Kate kept her stocked up with wine, crisps and other necessities more important than milk or biscuits, while Callie's mother had packed the freezer full of home-made lasagnes and fish pies when she had refused the offer to go back and stay with her parents until she was better.

"But, darling, you would be much better off away from it all. Somewhere where you can forget about that dreadful man and what might have happened. It's not healthy to want to stay here, on your own," her mother had argued and Callie could tell that her father agreed but wouldn't push his opinion on her.

"I want to stay here. I want to remember, I want to feel angry, it's my way of healing," she told them firmly, although she wasn't sure she was right; she just didn't seem to be able to find the energy to do anything, even think. "Besides, I've got the move to plan," she'd told them and they had reluctantly agreed.

At least she was able to get dressed now. For the first few days she had just stayed on the sofa, curled up in a duvet, with Kate keeping close and caring for her. Miller had visited several times, and it was these visits that had spurred her on to get up, washed and dressed, and to give Kate the confidence to go back to work.

"How was it in court?" she asked him, as she handed him a cup of coffee. Gerry Brown had been appearing in front of magistrates pending review of his ongoing custody. Samuel had told her that he was pretty sure the GMC would be taking him off the medical register permanently if he was found guilty. Not if, she told herself, when.

"Remanded," he answered and she could feel the relief course through her veins, even though she hadn't been aware that it would mean so much to her. She felt her knees buckle and the coffee slopped on the work surface.

"Woah!" Miller said and grabbed hold of her, supporting her. "Let's get you over to a chair."

His strong arms around her, he began to help her towards the sofa. She looked up at him, tilting her head and he stopped walking and looked into her eyes. Slowly, carefully lest she objected, he lowered his head down to hers and kissed her. It was a long lingering kiss and when he tried to break away, she put her hand around his neck and pulled him back to her, to her lips and let herself melt against him.

There was the sound of a key turning in the lock and Callie pushed away from Miller's embrace, from his kiss, just as Billy walked in.

"Oh, sorry," he said, standing in the doorway looking at the pair of them. "I've still got a key," he explained showing them the bunch in his hand. "I didn't mean to interrupt anything, I just wanted to see how you were, after, well, everything."

Callie looked at the bag he had dropped at his feet and he followed her gaze.

"It's over," he said awkwardly. "Alison and me."

There was an awkward pause as Callie desperately tried to think what to say, what she felt about him coming back expecting to just pick up where he had left off. Primarily, she felt anger, but, but...

"I can always find a hotel," he said.

"That's okay," Callie said as Miller moved away from her. She couldn't bring herself to look at him; she didn't want to see how he felt about their kiss, or Billy arriving. Harsh as it was, she didn't want his feelings to colour any decision she might make. "We have a lot we need to discuss."

THE END

If you enjoyed this book, please let others know by leaving a quick review on Amazon. Also, if you spot anything untoward in the paperback, get in touch. We strive for the best quality and appreciate reader feedback.

editor@thebookfolks.com

www.thebookfolks.com

DEAD PRETTY – Book 1

When a woman is found dead in Hastings, Sussex, the medical examiner feels a murder has taken place. Yet she feels the police are not doing enough because the victim is a prostitute. Dr Callie Hughes will conduct her own investigation, no matter the danger.

BODY HEAT – Book 2

A series of deadly arson attacks piques the curiosity of Hastings police doctor Callie Hughes. Faced with police incompetence, once again she tries to find the killer herself, but her meddling won't win her any favours and in fact puts her in a compromising position.

GUILTY PARTY – Book 3

A lawyer in a twist at his home. Another dead in a private pool. Someone has targeted powerful individuals in the coastal town of Hastings. Dr Callie Hughes uses her medical expertise to find the guilty party.

VITAL SIGNS – Book 4

When bodies of migrants begin to wash up on the Sussex coast, police doctor Callie Hughes has the unenviable task of inspecting them. But one body stands out to her as different. Convinced that finding the victim's identity will help crack the people smuggling ring, she decides to start her own investigation.

DEADLY REMEDIES – Book 5

When two elderly individuals pass away, it is not an unusual occurrence for seaside town doctor and medical examiner Callie Hughes. But she notices that both of the deceased had a suitcase packed, and her suspicions are aroused. Who is the killer that is prematurely taking them to their final destination?

MURDER LUST – Book 6

After noticing strange marks on the body of a woman found dead in a holiday let, police doctor Callie Hughes probes further. The police take her concerns about a serial killer seriously, but achieve little when another body if found. Callie is possibly the only obstacle to the murderer getting away with the crime, and that makes her a potential target.

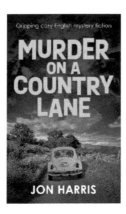

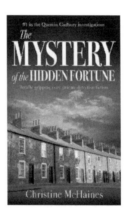

THE MYSTERY OF THE HIDDEN FORTUNE
by Christine McHaines

Quentin Cadbury, a useless twenty-something, is left to look
after his late aunt's London house when his parents head to
Australia. But burglars seem determined to break in, and not
even the stray cat he befriends can help him. As the thieves
are after something pretty valuable, and illegal, he must
grow up pretty fast to get out of a sticky situation.

For more great books, visit www.thebookfolks.com

Printed in Great Britain
by Amazon

34298944R00112